Linda
6

2014
2

Timing

Lori Bell

This book is a work of fiction. Names, characters, places and incidents are the product of the author's imagination or are used fictitiously. Any resemblance to actual events, locales, or persons, living or dead, is coincidental.

Copyright © 2014 by Lori Bell

All rights reserved. This book or any portion thereof may not be reproduced or used in any manner whatsoever without the express written permission of the publisher except for the use of brief quotations in a book review.

Cover photograph by Lori Bell
Photographed in red stilettos, model Abigail Haag

http://www.sparrowspointcc.org/
http://www.livestrong.com/article/66468-tylenol-toxicity-symptoms/
http://community.babycenter.com/post/a29334391/visitors_in_nicu
http://www.nblawgroup.com/practice-areas/car-truck-accidents/common-car-accident-injuries/

Printed by CreateSpace

ISBN 978-1502568175

DEDICATION

For all of you who believe everything happens for a reason.

CHAPTER 1

Tasha Wheelan was inside of her parked car, sunglasses on, sitting low behind the wheel. It didn't matter how deep she sunk down into her seat or if she wore bulky sunglasses to hide her face. Her car would give her away if he saw it.

She had never done this before. Followed him. She felt like a spy. A private investigator sounded classier to her. And classy is her style. Her clothes are expensive, her nails are regularly manicured, her toes pedicured, and her naturally brown hair gets highlighted a little bit more blonde every few weeks. Tasha is forty-five years old and fighting to keep her body looking twenty years younger. Daily workouts at the gym, cleansing diets, starvation. She attempts it all. She has to. For him. To keep him.

Lori Bell

Why is she doing this? Her mind raced. Her heart felt heavy. Heavier than usual. Why now? And what is she going to do differently if Harrison Wheelan walks out to his car, parked overnight in that five-star hotel's parking lot, and sees her.

They have been married nearly twenty years and share two children. Their daughter, Ari is nineteen and a freshman in college in New York City, where the Wheelans are originally from. When their family moved to Baltimore, Maryland two and a half years ago, no one wholeheartedly wanted to make the change. Especially not Ari. She wanted to graduate from high school with all of her friends, the peers she had grown up with since prekindergarten. Her ten-year-old brother, Spence was also apprehensive about leaving the only home and friends he too had ever known. Tasha encouraged her children to be supportive of their father's once-in-a-lifetime opportunity to spearhead his own law practice. He and a colleague took a leap of faith and it had been one profitable move. So profitable that Tasha had yet to introduce Baltimore to her home interior design business which reaped its own share of profit for fifteen years in New York City. Her children were her main focus when they moved. She wanted to see them through this life change. Their concerns and their fears were also hers. Little did Ari and Spence know that it was their mother who would have the most to lose when their family moved to Baltimore.

Timing

Harrison called her when she had dinner warming in the oven the night before. He was going to be working late again, *probably all night because his latest case isn't going to solve itself,* he told her. And she wanted to believe him. Always. She loves him, and the idea that he is having an affair is not something she is going to allow herself to fathom. He loves her. Or so he used to tell her. Things are different between them now. And that has been the vibe for a very long time. Back in New York City, her work kept her mind from dwelling. Dwelling on the fact that she and her husband no longer share any intimacy. He used to love her like crazy, and she never could tear herself apart from him. It was a fairytale love. Between them. The two of them had absolutely nothing when they got married, both twenty-five years old. Nothing but each other. And how ironic it felt now to have all of the money and material things – the enormous house, the fancy cars, closets full of designer clothes and shoes, and a special drawer full of jewelry – but to feel so poor. So empty. So lost.

And that is why when she woke up this morning, to find his side of the bed undisturbed because he had not slept there again, she decided it is time to find out the truth. Time to confront him. She took a shower, blow-dried her shoulder-length hair, and pulled it up on top of her head into a loose bun. After applying all of her makeup, she slipped into a straight sleeveless peach dress which ended well above the knees, and nude heels. She added a finishing touch around her neck with a chunky gold necklace. All dressed up to drive her son to school and then find her husband.

Lori Bell

Tasha drove to his law firm. His car was absent from the parking lot. Harrison has his own parking spot, right in front of the building. It was nine o'clock in the morning. *Maybe he went back home for a shower and a change of clothes after working all night? Maybe I should stop giving him the benefit of the doubt and start doubting him? Start asking questions.* Tasha's mind was reeling as she drove to her husband's favorite five-star hotel in the city of Baltimore. She had seen the name of it on their credit card statement before. It was the location of one of his favorite dining spots. The *buffet is wonderful,* he would tell her. He took her and the kids there for brunch last Mother's Day. And he was right about the food.

And that is exactly where she found his car today. Her car was running, the air conditioner vents were blowing directly onto her face and bare arms. She was trying to cool down as she stared at the back of his silver BMW, parked directly in front of her black one. His and Hers. Theirs. Their cars. Their life. *It sure as hell didn't feel like they shared much of anything these days,* she was thinking. Dwelling. Stewing.

But she did love him. And that is why she shifted her car into reverse, backed out of the parking spot, and drove away from that hotel. And away from the chance she decided not to take.

***

Timing

She drove too fast down the city streets as she felt angry and disappointed. Why did he have that effect on her? Why couldn't she bring herself to face him, confront him, accuse him? If she was the one not coming home at night, he would question her and demand the truth. And that is pretty much who they had become as husband and wife. Harrison Wheelan made the demands and his wife obliged. In return, she lived a life of luxury.

What more could she want? *Nothing*, she thought to herself. *I don't want for anything. But I need so much more. I need to feel loved by my husband, the man who used to talk to me, touch me and hold me and want me. Only me.*

Tears were welling up in her eyes as she reached her destination. She always ended up there. The one person who always listened and then gave her treasured advice was now only able to listen. At least Tasha had hoped she was listening. As Tasha walked through the grass, she gave herself a mental reminder not to wear heels on the days she visited the cemetery. It was a challenge to walk on top of that uneven ground, and today the grass was in dire need of mowing. The already hot May sun was beating on her bare, tan shoulders as she stood in front of her mother's tombstone with an overwhelming need to have a heart-to-heart conversation with the one person who always understood her. Tasha's father abandoned her and her mother when she was nine years old and her mother never remarried. When Tasha and her family moved to Baltimore, her mother lasted one month in New York City before she too decided to move to be close to her daughter and her grandchildren. She rented an apartment in the city of Baltimore, just ten minutes away from Tasha and her family. She only lived in that apartment for three weeks before she died. A drunk driver hit her head on, in broad daylight. She had been driving from the gym she just joined at Tasha's urging. *Mom, it will be a great way to stay in shape and meet a few people, make some friends.* Mary Collins was sixty-five years old and gone from this world in the blink of an eye. And Tasha's world has not been the same since. Losing her mother still felt surreal more than two years later. The shock of how it had happened would stay with Tasha for the rest of her life. And the pain had yet to lessen.

Tasha reached up to her face and removed her sunglasses. "Hi Mom... I guess you know why I'm here." Tasha's mother had known how strained her daughter's marriage had become over the years. She called it *unhealthy* to live like they were, but Tasha never had the courage to make a change for the better. "I don't know what comes over me. I was so close, but I couldn't do it." Tasha was about to continue speaking softly, standing on the ground above where her mother's body was buried, when she heard a weed trimmer nearby and she saw a man working his way around the tombstones. It would only be minutes before he would want to manicure the ground near her mother's grave. She wasn't ready to leave. She had just gotten there. Tasha was feeling annoyed. She wanted to continue talking to her mother in hopes of seeking some direction from beyond, but she was uncomfortable talking knowing she was no longer alone out there. A few minutes passed as Tasha rearranged the flowers on the grave which she brought with her last week when she visited. As she squatted down in her dress and heels, the trimming stopped and the man who disrupted her concentration stood in the row of tombstones directly across from her. And then he spoke to her.

"I'm sorry, ma'am, I don't mean to be rude but I have to tend to the trimming out here this morning." He was being polite, Tasha realized, but calling her ma'am made her feel old. He may have been about eight or ten years younger than her, but still, *leave the ma'am out of it*. Tasha looked over at him as she stood up, trying to be graceful in heels that were digging into the soft soil and in a dress too short for squatting. He was wearing faded jeans that molded to the tight muscles in his thighs, tan work boots, and a sleeveless white t-shirt. His toned arms were every bit as tan as hers but she is certain his golden color came from the natural sunlight, unlike hers from the tanning bed at the beauty salon. His light brown hair, with sun streaks of blond, nearly covered his eyes. He could have used a haircut but looking unkept seemed like his style, Tasha thought as she answered him. "You're not being rude, and I can see that you all are more than a few days behind on taking care of the grounds out here." Her comment was a little too blunt and incredibly snooty sounding, but he didn't seem to mind.

"I'm Jack, and you are?" He walked closer and stood only a couple inches taller than her, but she was wearing her two-inch heels out there in the grass. At barely five foot three, she loved wearing heels. And being coupled with Harrison at six-foot-two, Tasha did what she could to keep it from looking like he towered over her.

"Natasha Wheelan, and this is my mother's grave. Do you have a last name, Jack?" Tasha smirked when she asked him that, and she wondered why in the hell she did ask. *She really didn't care about Jack's last name.*

"Yes, Natasha, I do. It's Williams." Jack Williams stood in the tall grass behind the stone that bore Tasha's mother's name.

"Well Jack Williams, I better let you get back to work. I can come back tomorrow." Tasha started to back away to leave when Jack spoke again.

"We all need our mamas, I'm very sorry for your loss." His words were sincere and they touched her to her core. She felt something so powerful at that moment, she felt understood, and she instantly wanted to stay. "Thank you, Jack." She was no longer a woman dressed to the nines, hiding behind flawless makeup, riding on her high horse. He had immediately seen right through her, past the fancy clothes and unreachable persona. She seemed real to him, and he too wanted her to stay. "She had to have been young when she died," Jack said peeking around to look at the date on the stone, "because you are just a baby yourself, Natasha."

"She was sixty-five, and I'm hardly a baby, and you can call me Tasha," she grinned as she said it and he returned a sweet smile to her.

"Well, let's see, I'm thirty-six so I'm guessing you are six months or maybe a year wiser than I am?" This time Tasha giggled at him and he brushed the hair out of his eyes and wiped the sweat off of his brow with the back of his bare hand. His face was also sun-kissed and his features were striking, so masculine. Tasha was staring at his strong cheekbones and jawline.

"Try nine years wiser, you suck up," Tasha was joking with him. A stranger who she so suddenly felt incredibly comfortable with. This is ridiculous, she thought, but she liked how this felt with him. She was flirting, and she knew it, but that feeling had been absent to her for so long she was just going with it. *What did she have to lose? It's not like she would ever see this man again.*

"Suck up?" Jack laughed out loud, "Now why in the world would I be sucking up to a fancy pants little girl like you? So what's your story anyway? Shouldn't you be at work or at the country club dressed like that?"

"Probably, but I had a stop to make first," Tasha replied, thinking that, first, she is not a little girl. She is just petite. And second, she and Harrison do belong to a private, member-owned country club, located in southeastern Baltimore County. The club sat on two hundred and seventy-two acres of natural woodlands and waterways which overlooked the scenic Chesapeake Bay tributaries. The golf course there ranks among some of the most challenging in Maryland, and Harrison practically lived there on the weekends. It is a full service clubhouse for both formal and casual dining and parties, and Tasha is partial to the main dining room with a copper fireplace and the impressive waterfront view overlooking Bear Creek.

"You looked very serious standing over here when you first walked up, I hope everything is okay in your life," Jack offered, and Tasha thought to herself how everything is not okay in her life and has not been for a very long time.

"Oh I'm fine, it just makes me sad having to pay a visit to my mother...here." Tasha really didn't have anyone to talk to privately and on such a personal level anymore. Not since she lost her mother. And not since she moved from New York City, leaving behind a few girlfriends and losing touch with them except for an occasional text or keeping up with their lives through the newsfeed on Facebook.

"Well I don't like to see anyone sad but that unfortunately goes with the job when working out here," Jack said, bending down to pull a few weeds from around Mary Collins' marker of life.

"So this is your job?" Tasha asked, "Cemetery

Timing

groundskeeper?" She wondered how in the world a man could survive on that income, or if he had a family to support. Money had not been a concern for Tasha for so very long, she had pretty much forgotten what it felt like to live paycheck to paycheck and even rob Peter to pay Paul, as the story in the Catholic bible goes.

"This, actually, is my father's job. He lives on the grounds," Jack pointed to the modest two-story home on the hill in the distance, "and I'm just helping him out right now. It's hard to find good help out here."

"Well that's very kind of you," Tasha said, wondering if Jack has a *real* job. Her place in society, she thought, allowed her to pass judgment on others. She knew being a groundskeeper is indeed a real job that requires labor in any kind of weather, but she simply had not been impressed.

"I really should get back to work, you know, get the grounds cleaned up today...so you can come back tomorrow and not have to fight the weeds in your expensive heels," Jack said, looking at her and she did feel a bit silly all dolled up out there.

"Of course. I need to get going anyway. Maybe I'll see you tomorrow, Jack Williams?" she asked as she started to walk away and heard him say, "I'll be here."

***

Lori Bell

When she pulled into the three-car garage of their immense four-thousand square-foot home with all white brick, she opened her car door and swung her legs out before taking off her dirty heels. She walked barefoot on the immaculate garage floor, over to the large basin in the corner. She ran water from the faucet over her heels and rinsed both clean before drying them with paper towels she retrieved from the holder hanging on the wall above the sink. Then she walked into the house and entered the kitchen. There weren't enough dishes to put into the dishwasher. Spence is the only one who had eaten breakfast, just a bowl of cereal. She looked out of the window at the view of their spacious backyard, lined with trees, bushes, and flowers in the rock landscape. Her concentration was broken at the sound of a riding lawn mower starting up. The Wheelans hired a lawn service to take care of their yard and three young men were now there to do that. Tasha immediately thought of Jack Williams, working hard in the hot sun on the cemetery grounds. Her next thought led her upstairs into her daughter's room. Ari had packed and taken most of her clothes and belongings with her to college, but Tasha did manage to find a pair of cut-off jean shorts, over-frayed on the ends, and then she walked into her own bedroom and found a plain white tank top that she sometimes wore to the gym. She quickly took off her dress and threw it onto the end of the bed. She easily slipped into the jean shorts as she and Ari are now wearing the same size, in clothes and in shoes. Ari, since the start of college, had actually gained a few pounds and is now slightly heavier

Timing

than her mother. Tasha herself could afford to gain weight too, but she wasn't about to allow that to happen. Now in her tank and shorts, Tasha grabbed her tennis shoes which she always wore to the gym, and a pair of no-show black ankle socks as she walked out of her bedroom and downstairs to the garage. Her hair was still up, her sunglasses were back on, as she backed out the driveway and drove away.

Any other day she would have gotten a mani-pedi, a highlight, or shopped the hours away at the mall. Today, however, she felt different and she was going to go with that feeling. It was time to mix things up a little bit. She was ready to step outside of her stuffy box. If only for a little while.

When she drove back onto the cemetery grounds, she saw him on a riding mower. His back was to her until she had almost walked directly up to him. When he turned the wheel and saw her, for a moment he didn't recognize her in those clothes. Everyday clothes, to him. But then he saw her hair still up, her face still painted, and of course her fancy car parked not too far from where she stood before him.

"What in the name of God have you done to yourself?" he asked her after he shut off the motor. "You almost look ready to get your hands dirty....maybe even break a sweat!" He was teasing her and certainly wondering why she came back. He hadn't been able to think about much else since she left and said she would return tomorrow.

CHAPTER 2

When she said she wanted to help, Jack initially thought she was going to be a handful for him. More trouble than she might be worth. He certainly wanted to give her a chance though, and three hours later the grounds were immaculate again. All of the grass was mowed, all of the tedious trimming around each grave was done, and the flowers on top of every stone were back in place. Jack never could have done it in one day without Tasha's help, once she caught on to how to operate the mower and the trimmer, and he told her exactly that while they sat beneath a large oak tree for a break. He handed her a bottle of water from his small cooler and the triangular-shaped half of his turkey, lettuce and cheese sandwich with both mayonnaise and mustard slathered on it.

Timing

"First of all, I don't think there was a rush to get anything out here done in one day, and second I can't eat your lunch," Tasha said, refusing to take the sandwich half. "Please," he said, "It's the least I can do, and you must be hungry." Tasha changed her mind and took the sandwich from him. Her hand brushed his and it had felt calloused in places and soft in others. "And, no, I am not in a rush but I do appreciate your help, Tasha." The way he said her name made her smile. "I needed this today more than you know," she said, taking a bite of the sandwich before she continued, "I am married with two children and quite honestly I don't know who I am anymore or where I fit in." This was the most honest she had been with anyone in such a long time. Especially herself.

Jack was listening intently. He knew something was troubling her this morning, but he didn't want to pry. He did want to know more about her so he kept silent, hoping she would continue. "I'm probably giving you too much information, given the fact that we are strangers," Tasha said and he added, "Sometimes it's easier to talk to strangers. Most won't be so quick to judge you. I know I won't."

Tasha smiled at him and said, "Thanks, Jack," as they both took long drinks from their chilled bottles of water. Jack also had an apple, a banana, and a small plastic baggie full of purple grapes that he shared with her while she did most of the talking. She told him about herself and her family originally being from New York. She filled him in on the ages of her children and confessed to missing her daughter who is away at college. She saved the story of Harrison for last.

"So you think your husband is cheating on you... but you haven't confronted him?" Jack looked confused and Tasha nodded her head, feeling ashamed of being such a coward. Jack could see the pain in her eyes and he was hoping to find the right words to say to her. "I think everything happens for a reason," he told her. "Maybe you are not ready to lose him or to give up on your marriage. I can understand that, but I do want you to know that living in limbo like you're telling me you have been doing for a very long time is not fair to you, or to your children."

"My children are happy," Tasha defended.

"But you're not, are you?" Jack bluntly asked her, and she hesitated to answer him. She had everything her heart desired in the form of material things. And it was beyond important to her for her children to be healthy and happy and she felt blessed because they are. But, now, after just one day of doing something entirely out of her element, she felt productive and alive again. She felt like she had so much more inside of her to offer, to give back.

Timing

She felt like she deserved to be appreciated and loved again. She and Harrison had a wonderful, loving, solid relationship before. If only they could get that back again.

"No, not like I know I could be. I mean, I used to be happy and comfortable in my own skin." Jack was looking at her, really looking at her. Her mascara was smeared under her eyes, her forehead was sticky and damp from sweating, and her hair was windblown. She hardly looked like the same woman all gussied up who he had met just hours earlier. He was looking at a real woman now. "Well you look damn good in that skin, and I'm not coming on to you with a line. I'm telling you because I think it's safe to say we became friends today. And that's what friends do, lift each other up, right?"

"I work my ass off to stay in a size four and look good in my forties. Today was the first time I ate a fucking sandwich in five years," Tasha laughed out loud at her own comment and Jack joined her. "I'll bet you don't cuss like a sailor much either," he added and she blushed because he had her figured out. And then she grew serious again, "Most women would envy me, but you know what Jack... they don't know my heart."

Jack looked at her with concern in his eyes. "It's none of my business what you do with the doubts and fears you have in your marriage, but I'm hoping you will do what makes you happy. And I'm also hoping this isn't the last I see of you, Tasha Wheelan."

"Are you offering me a job, Jack Williams?" Tasha teased him. She had to say something to break the mood between them which had suddenly gotten entirely too serious. And he laughed. "How about lunch any day you choose to assist me on these grounds? My father is sick and needs a few months to get back on his feet, God willing, so I will be here handling all of this myself."

"I just might stop by, if you're lucky," Tasha teased him again. And then she helped him gather the trash from their lunch under the shade tree.

***

Tasha left the cemetery just in time to pick up Spence from school. He did a double-take at her when he got into the car. She was still wearing Ari's cut-off shorts and her white tank top was stained from spending the day working outside. "Mom, what happened to you?" Spence asked, giggling at her as he buckled his seatbelt and placed his backpack at his feet.

"Well I just came from the cemetery and grandma's grave needed a little work done around it." That was a good enough excuse for her son, but he still glanced at her a few times during their drive home. She looked different to him. She was always wearing dresses or designer

Timing

clothes, and her hair and makeup were always perfect. Today, he thought, she looked younger and fun. And he was right.

***

Tasha was surprised to learn from Spence that Harrison would be home in time for his baseball game tonight. Spence was scheduled to pitch and he wanted his dad there. Her husband had not told her. Harrison is a good father, very involved with his children, especially with their sports and extracurricular activities. If Tasha had allowed herself, she could have easily become jealous of the attention her children received from Harrison. But, she loved seeing him show interest and genuine concern and love for both Ari and Spence. She just wanted to be on the receiving end of some of that again.

While Spence was upstairs in his bedroom changing into his baseball uniform, Tasha was quickly heating some leftover roast beef in au ju sauce in the microwave and getting the bread out of the cabinet to make her son an open-faced sandwich before he had to be on the baseball field for warm ups. Tasha was hurrying, hoping to be able to take a quick shower or at least freshen up and change clothes while her son ate. She was still wearing her cut-offs and she wasn't about to go to her son's game looking ragged.

The sandwich was hot and ready as she called her son into the kitchen, but he wasn't the one who walked in. It was Harrison, entering the room through the garage. She had not heard his car pull in.

"Hi, you startled me, Spence told me you wanted to make it to his game and I'm about to feed him and get him there." Tasha was busy setting a place at the table for her son when she turned around to find Harrison staring at her.

"What are you wearing?" he asked her, wondering how she spent her day, but he didn't ask her. He knew how she spent her free time. At the gym. At the mall. At the beauty salon. He thought his wife was beautiful, but she had become too superficial to him over the years. He actually missed the woman she used to be. And something had just stirred inside of him, seeing her dressed so casual and looking carefree. But he, again, wasn't about to tell her that. The open communication, compliments, playful banter, all were lost between them and had been for a very long time.

"Oh, yeah, this," Tasha said, looking down at her clothing and wishing she had taken the time to change her clothes before Harrison came home. "I spent some time at mom's grave today and pulled a few weeds." She wasn't going to tell him that she actually drove a riding lawn more and used a weed eater, both for the first time in her

Timing

life. She also would leave out the fact that she made a new friend today. Harrison never gave her the chance to say anything further as he shrugged his shoulders in his long-sleeved white dress shirt and red print tie, and he immediately turned his attention to his son who walked into the room wearing his royal blue and white baseball uniform. Tasha slipped out of the room then to put herself together for the game. When she walked away, Harrison may have been listening to Spence's excitement about the game, but his eyes were on his wife. She looked different, no doubt, but for the first time in what seemed like forever, he had taken notice of her.

***

Spence was already in the dugout when Tasha and Harrison retrieved their lawn chairs from the trunk of the car and walked up to the crowd of parents already there. Harrison was walking three or four feet in front of her. He always led the way. Took charge. She wished, just once, he would walk alongside of her or allow her to lead the way. Ladies first. Once both of their lawn chairs were open, Tasha was about to sit down with him when he walked away from her. He spotted someone he knew and he began talking baseball or something else and left his wife sitting alone. For the entire game.

At times, she would glance over at him, feeling her eyes welling up with tears behind her sunglasses. But she didn't cry. She is stronger than that. She should be used to this. He had no interest in sitting next to her, being with her, cheering on their son together. Tasha took pictures of Spence with her iPhone, and smiled at him as if all was well whenever he made eye contact with her, and she casually spoke to a few of the other moms who were seated near her. She was insulted by Harrison tonight. Her husband. She knew the people around her witnessed the two of them walk up together, only to see Harrison abandon her immediately and all throughout the nine innings, eventually even sitting down on the bleachers with a few other guys. *Son of a bitch.* She thought to herself, more than once. *How could he do this to her? And why is she putting up with the way he treats her?*

***

After they were at home and getting ready for bed, Tasha walked into their master bedroom to find Harrison wearing black silk pajama pants very low on his waist as he stood on the side of the bed, removing the decorative pillows and shams in order to pull the covers back and climb in. His chest was bare and fit because he too is a gym rat. Tasha noticed his farmer's tan from the polo shirts he wears while golfing, and his jet-black hair still looked damp from the shower and she could see specks of gray all throughout it. He is aging well and looking very distinguished, Tasha thought to herself as she stared at him, wondering where they went wrong, how they lost their connection. *Do all people who find fortune lose sight of what is really important?* It was silly that something so simple as cleaning up the cemetery grounds had made Tasha realize today how much she missed being real. Maybe it wasn't that at all. Maybe it was Jack Williams. Tasha tried to erase the image of him with his long bangs in his eyes, his tan skin glistening with sweat, as she slipped into bed beside her husband, wearing a short pink spaghetti strap nightgown. She didn't want any other man. She wanted the one lying beside her.

Harrison had already turned off the light in their bedroom and when Tasha spoke to him in the dark, she felt braver with him than she had in a very long time. "Does it feel good to sleep in your own bed tonight?" she asked him, wondering if he was in bed with another woman last night. Or ever before.

"It feels good to know I will be getting sleep. Period. I worked all night last night, showered at the gym before I had a breakfast meeting at The Sierra, and then put in another full day." There it was. An explanation for why his car had been parked at that hotel.

"I'm glad you're home tonight, Harry." She hadn't called him Harry in so long. It was her pet name for him.

Years ago. He already had his back to her and remained turned away from her as he pulled the covers up over his bare shoulders and replied, "Me too. Goodnight."

CHAPTER 3

The next morning after Tasha brought Spence to school, she went back home. She needed to come up with a plan for dinner and either get something cooking in the crock-pot or make sure she had ingredients to make a meal later. She planned to be gone all day. She was going to the mall. This was a different trip for her. She hadn't thought about getting her nails done in between department store browsing, she didn't want a new dress or another fancy pair of heels. She wanted to buy some every day clothes, as Jack Williams had called them, and she wanted to change the way she was spending her days. Starting now.

Lori Bell

She walked by Spence's bedroom and peeked her head in, noticing he had remembered to make his own bed this morning. She was impressed because she had yet to make her own. When she pulled up the sheets and straightened out the duvet on her bed, Tasha thought about the night before. Last night she wanted her husband. To hold her. To love her. She hardly slept at all, she was just lying there thinking and wondering and wishing and hoping. And finally, praying. At first, her prayer began with talking to her mother in heaven. She, once again, needed her guidance. Then, she turned to God. And now she was remembering that prayer. *I know I do not talk to you enough...you may think I only turn to you when I'm in a panic and need something to happen now. And you're probably right. I do need your help with something, but it doesn't have to happen right now. Just put me on the right path. I need my husband back. Just bring him back to me, God. I feel like my eyes have been opened. I have not been living my life the way I should. I know what is important now. Please God, help me to save my marriage.*

Tasha decided on making one of Harrison's favorites for dinner, a meatloaf. She turned her nose up just thinking about it and already knew she would be making something else on the side for herself and Spence. She planned to make a chocolate pie for dessert too. Another favorite of Harrison's. She was going to get him back by showing him how much she cared and making

Timing

him feel loved again. But she was ignoring the obvious fact. She still loves him for sure, but did he still love her? She felt last night was her first attempt in a very long time to reach out to him, but he rejected her. *Did she try hard enough?* Well tonight she is going to try harder.

***

Spence ended up requesting a grilled cheese sandwich and a can of tomato soup. He was in a hurry to eat and run. It was Friday night and he was invited to a sleepover. He did not have a baseball game scheduled until Sunday afternoon, so Tasha gave him permission to stay overnight with a friend. While he was eating, he told his mom about his day at school.

"So I have a D in math and Mrs. Klutho is probably going to be calling you." Spence has always been her straightforward child. He knew he could talk to his mom about anything. Ari is an altogether different child. Different personality. She is a hard nut to crack, for Tasha. She is her father's daughter. Tasha and Spence are connected and she appreciated that boy and his honestly and directness more than he will ever know.

"Spence, you know a D in any subject is unacceptable, especially if you want to remain on the baseball team," Tasha was sitting across from her son, watching him slurp his soup on a hot weather day and she wondered why he was even craving it. He had her brownish-blond hair and her hazel eyes and sweet smile. At ten years old he was still small, well under five foot and only weighing seventy-two pounds, but she knew one day he would be as tall as Harrison. Ari was already taller than her, so Tasha expected to remain the pipsqueak in their household.

"I know, mom, and I'm going to need your help with math homework to get that grade up fast, before the end of the school year."

"I will do what I can, but you have to promise to apply yourself," Tasha said, trying to be serious while looking at his sweet face with tomato soup and bread crumbs on his mouth and chin. "Use your napkin, buddy," she added and he did while he asked her a question that completely threw her for a loop.

"So you made dad's favorite meatloaf tonight....Does that mean you still love him?" Their children had never before seemed concerned about the relationship that had, little by little, lost its steam over the years.

"Why would you ask me that, Spence? Of course I love your dad. I always have."

"But the two of you are so, I don't know, distant is the word I guess," Spence began to explain, "and I saw

Timing

how hurt you were the other night at my game when dad left you sitting there, alone."

This is where she could have tried to cover up her feelings, brush off her son's observation as being silly or nothing at all to worry about. But she didn't. She treasured his honesty and wanted to give him the same. Always. "Oh Spence, my sweet, sensitive, boy. Yes, I was hurt and I'm going to do everything I can to reconnect with your dad. He and I live in the same house and we once shared so much love. I am going to get that back for us, for all of us. I want you and Ari to feel like we all are a real family again."

***

Spence was already at his friend's house for a sleepover when Tasha had just finished preparing a salad with romaine lettuce for herself and Harrison. She also had two baked potatoes individually wrapped in aluminum foil, warming in the oven. She intended to eat a baked potato and a salad with no dressing and skip the meatloaf. It was five-thirty and Tasha was hoping this wouldn't be one of those late nights at the office for her husband. He always called her to let her know and she had not heard from him. She was going to sit down at the table and wait for him when she heard the garage door opening. She wished herself good luck and took a deep breath. *Here goes my chance... to put the spark back into my marriage.*

Harrison walked through the garage and entered the house through the kitchen door. The first thing he noticed is he and his wife were alone. He always found it easier to greet his son and pay attention to him first. The next thing he took notice of is his wife, wearing short khaki shorts and a fitted pale pink v-neck t-shirt. The material was thin and he could see her white lacy bra through it. He was staring as he managed to say, "Hi, dinner smells great."

Tasha smiled at him. "It's just you and me tonight. Spence is already off to a sleepover. I made a meatloaf..."

"Really? Gosh when was the last time I had meatloaf in this house? You don't even like meatloaf." He remembered and that instantly made her feel hopeful. This was starting off well. And she hoped the rest of the night would follow suit. She grinned to herself as she thought about when the kids were younger and her mom would let them sleep over at her house. She and Harrison would call those nights, *sleepover sex*, and they always took advantage of an empty house. She could not remember the last time they made love. Maybe only two or three times since they moved to Baltimore nearly three years ago. The most recent time Harrison had come home late after having golfed all day and drinking one too many

Timing

beers with the guys. The kids were asleep and she had been sitting up in their bed reading, but not really concentrating on her book. She was waiting for him. Worried about him. When he walked into their bedroom she could see him stumbling around to take off his clothes and he was way too happy for Harrison. She was glad he made it home safe in that condition and when she told him so, he came on to her. Strong. When it was over she wasn't sure if she ever wanted him to touch her again. Their lovemaking had felt so much more to her like assault rather than affection. He had torn her favorite silver satin nightgown that night. His hands on her, his mouth on her. She wanted him again now, but she wanted the gentle Harrison she remembered. So gentle sometimes he had driven her crazy, touching her, enticing her. He did it on purpose. He wanted to see her eyes roll back, and hear her moans almost turn into cries. He loved the control he had over her.

"It's been awhile, I know," Tasha replied. "I thought you would enjoy it. I think it's time we both get back to enjoying the simpler things in life. And each other, again." Harrison was taking off his yellow print tie and he hung it over one of the empty chairs at the kitchen table. He didn't respond to what she had just told him, but he wondered what was going on with her lately. Her clothes were casual, and she never dressed casual. She hadn't in a very long time. And now she definitely had him thinking.

Lori Bell

The small talk between them was good all throughout dinner and when she was loading the dishwasher, Harrison walked out of the room. Tasha knew she had to keep the communication going tonight. She hurried to clean up the kitchen and awhile later she found her husband dressed in gray gym shorts and a powder blue t-shirt. He had his no-show black athletic socks on and he was carrying his tennis shoes as he walked through their bedroom.

"Are you headed to the gym now?" Tasha asked him, feeling disappointed that he was leaving again.

"Yes I am, I didn't have time to work out at the office today so I want to go tonight. I know it will be packed on a Friday night, but we don't have anything else going on."

"Actually we do," Tasha spoke up. She was not going to be submissive anymore. She was not going to let him call the shots. *She wanted to make this work and dammit she wanted him to meet her halfway.* "Look Harrison, I'm really trying here," she said to him as they stood in the middle of their spacious master bedroom with all hardwood flooring, except for the large area rug placed underneath their bed. Their bed is an antique made of dark maple wood and it has four tall, thick round posts at each corner. It sits high off of the floor and being only five-foot-three, Tasha used to joke that she needed a stepladder

Timing

to get into bed. "I want to reconnect with you, I want our marriage back." She took a few steps toward him and he was giving her a blank stare. "We need to find each other again. I don't want to feel like strangers living under the same roof...and I want to share a bed with you again, the way we used to."

"What is going on here, Tasha? We are married. We do sleep in the same bed. Nothing has changed for me. I'm in a good place. I am a successful lawyer with a wife and two kids. That's where I am at."

Tasha wanted to feel offended. It was always about him. The fucking move to Baltimore, uprooting all of their lives was about him. Her own mother even changed her life to make that move, and then inevitably lost her life. "I want you to talk to me. We both need to reach out to each other, and treat each other with love and respect again. I love you, Harry..." And that's when she walked toward him and stood up on her toes and pressed her lips against his. She wanted him. So much. Here. Now. Right now.

He momentarily responded to her kiss as she reached her hand into his gym shorts and felt him. He didn't feel turned on, but she intended to help him get to that point. And quickly. She could feel the muscles between her own legs tightening. *God it's been too long.* His hands were on her shoulders and she stepped back and stood before him and took off her shirt and then her shorts. She stood there in her lacey white bra and matching thong. He was staring at her but had made no attempt to move closer, or to touch her. She reached behind her back and undid the clasp on her bra. "Touch me, Harry...make love to me, please." He didn't move so she dropped to her knees, pulled his shorts down enough to reach for him and attempt to take him into her mouth. His erection had grown and she was both excited and relieved to see she could still get to him, and please him. She found him with her tongue first. Then her lips. He was quiet and still but not resisting as she assumed he wanted this, so she slowly continued. And then he suddenly pulled away. And all she heard him say was, "I can't. I'm going to the gym."

    And when he walked out of their bedroom door, Tasha was sitting on the back of her legs on the hardwood floor. Her knees were still bent underneath her, but she could feel they were shaking. She didn't cry. She didn't get angry. She just felt like her heart was crumbling inside of her chest. At the same time, Harrison was backing out of the driveway in his car, overridden with guilt. He had already allowed another woman to do to him, just hours earlier, what his wife wanted to do just now. That is why he hadn't found the time to work out at the gym today. He sometimes closed and locked his office door. And that's where another woman had made him feel like a man today. A dishonest man.

CHAPTER 4

Tasha had to get out of the house, so she got dressed and left. She drove for awhile, up and down the city streets, through subdivisions. She wished she had somewhere to go. Someone to turn to. Her mother had always been that person for her. Tasha never really had a close girlfriend, just other women who she considered her casual friends. Acquaintances.

Finally, she stopped her car and got out at the cemetery. It was dark, graveside visiting hours were closed, but the property was well lit just in case anyone did feel the need to be close to a loved one. Was her mother really out there? No. Tasha believes Mary Collins is with her in spirit all of the time. There was just something about seeing her name on that tombstone. The day she was born. The day she so tragically left this earth. And this place was the final spot where Tasha had last seen her mother's body. So, in a way, she did feel like a part of her mother is in that ground below where she is standing.

"*Mom, I know what you would say to me tonight if you could... He is cheating on me. He wants to co-exist in the same house and in this so-called marriage, but he really doesn't need me. Or want me. I want to take Spence and leave, but he adores his father. I want to kick Harrison's ass out of the house because I deserve better. And...I want my husband back. Could I be any more confused here?*" Tasha sighed as she saw truck lights shining into the cemetery as one very loud, large diesel truck turned off of the highway and into the grounds. Tasha was annoyed at the interruption. *Who the hell comes out here this late at night?* Besides her.

And when the black truck stopped and parked close behind her car, she saw him get out. Jack Williams was wearing dark-washed denim, a tight white t-shirt, and faded, very worn brown cowboy boots. "You okay? You shouldn't be out here in the dark, all alone." Jack was happy to see her. He wondered if she would come back. Tasha had been in his thoughts and he hoped she would get her marriage back on track. If that is what she wants.

Timing

"I'm just talking to the one person who always had the right answers for me," Tasha tried to smile as Jack stepped closer to her in the grass. She could smell his cologne or aftershave or something which had suddenly filled the air when the wind picked up. "You're smelling good tonight, did you have a hot date or something?" It felt easy to joke with him. Her life is too serious at home.

"No," he responded, laughing, "not a hot date. I just came from the hospital. My father's recovery isn't going so well. He fell and broke his hip a month ago, had surgery and was on the mend. And now he has pneumonia. He's a stubborn fool and refused to get checked out at the doctor until I practically had to carry him to the ER tonight. He's gonna be set up in the hospital for a few days now."

"Oh my gosh, I'm sorry...you're a good son for all you do for him, taking care of the grounds out here and him." Tasha didn't know what more to say. She was being kind and honest, but she really didn't know this man all that well. She wondered what he did for a living. He obviously had put his life on hold to spend the summer living with his father. Tasha glanced at his left hand in the dark. No wedding ring.

"I'm all he has, it's the least I can do," And that is all Jack said about his father before he turned the attention back to Tasha. "I don't know what's going on with you tonight, but something brought you here and after the day

I had, I think we could both use a drink. Wanna come up to the house with me, for a beer?" First, Tasha didn't drink beer. She tried it once in her teens and simply hated the taste of it. She was more of a mixed drink, or glass of wine type. And second, what was she doing? *Well,* she thought to herself, *what did she have to lose?* Her son was at a sleepover and would not need her until morning. And her husband apparently didn't need or want her. "Sure. That sounds good."

Tasha got into her car and drove up the road which intertwined as it led up to the house on the hill. Jack had immediately passed her up as a signal for her to follow him in his loud and large truck. When they reached the old two-story white house with green shutters, Tasha thought of it as a well-kept home. She could tell, even in the dark, that Jack's father took pride in taking care of his home. And that home looked as immaculate inside as Tasha stepped through the front door when Jack held it open for her. It's been ages since Harrison held a door for her.

"Sorry, but you have to take off your shoes," Jack said, following her into the house. "My dad is anal about his floors staying clean." So as Jack stood with his back against the wall, to sturdy himself while he pulled off his boots, Tasha slipped off her white sandals with straps around the ankles and a slight heel and placed them side

Timing

by side on the WELCOME rug in front of the door. She was still wearing her khaki shorts and pink v-neck tee and with Jack now barefoot and in jeans and a white t-shirt, she felt casual and comfortable with him as she followed him into the kitchen and he took out two bottles of beer from the refrigerator. He twisted the caps off of both of them and handed one to her. She hesitated and smelled it first. This just wasn't her preference. And Jack noticed.

"You're not a beer drinker are you? I could look to see if my old man has any wine in the cellar," he offered and Tasha forced herself to take a swig of the cold beer. "I'm good, thanks," she said as she tried not to squint her eyes which were suddenly watering and then she forced herself to swallow hard. Jack didn't hide it. He laughed out loud at her and how she pretended to be into drinking that beer. She didn't fool him. She may have toned down her fancy attire, but she was still prissy. There was no way around that. "It's not medicine pretty girl, it's a beer. You're supposed to enjoy it, and want more." Tasha took another swig and pretended to relish in it. She actually didn't mind it the second time. And nearly ten minutes later, while sitting on a beige leather sofa in the living room with Jack, she had finished her first beer ever. Being just under five-foot-three and weighing one hundred and fifteen pounds, Tasha could always so easily get a buzz from alcohol. And tonight she had one as she began to explain to Jack what happened between her and Harrison just hours earlier.

"So my son is at a sleepover tonight, and I planned a romantic evening for my husband. I made a fucking gross meatloaf, his favorite, and I came on to him when he was getting ready to leave for the gym. What man refuses a blowjob?" Jack knew Tasha was loopy, which is partly why she was speaking so openly and so personally to him right now. He felt sympathy for her because even though he could hear the sarcasm in her voice, he saw the pain in her eyes. He also had to force himself not to go there in his mind. This woman, though almost ten years his senior, was beautiful and sexy and the idea of her on her knees with her mouth on his manhood instantly stirred him. In his thoughts. And in the skin between his legs.

"I don't know what to say... I'm sorry your husband is a dick," Jack's bluntness made Tasha giggle out loud and then she said, "Nice word choice," and he grinned at her and got up to get each of them another beer in the kitchen.

"I want your opinion," she said to him when he returned to the sofa with her. "You think my husband is having an affair, don't you?" Tasha took her first swig of her second beer, and this time she was past thinking she no longer disliked beer. Apparently she had quickly acquired a taste for it.

Timing

"I don't have a lot to go on, but from what you've told me about his late nights at the office, finding his car in a hotel parking lot, and turning down sex with his wife, I would say yes, that guy is getting it on with someone else." Tasha momentarily closed her eyes. She couldn't imagine it. She wouldn't allow herself to. But maybe it is time she does. Time to stop ignoring the obvious. She was hurting and Jack reached for her hand, which was placed on the cushion between them. He softly touched it, and again she could feel both the roughness and softness of his skin. His touch threw her a bit, so she pulled her hand away from his. "I'm sorry if I overstepped," he said in reference to touching her hand, but she replied in regards to him calling her husband an adulterer.

"No, it's okay. I want you to talk to me. I feel like I don't have a friend in the world anymore and I know I've found something like that, here with you," Tasha kept drinking and talking and she was again close to finishing another beer.

"Is that what you want from me, pretty girl? Friendship?" he asked her, staring at her. She was wearing her blonde-highlighted hair down tonight and it reached her shoulders.

"First, I'm not a girl... and what I want from you right now could make me a cougar, knowing you are too young for me." As she said those words, she made the first

41

move to put her lips on his. And unlike her husband just hours earlier, Jack Williams didn't resist her. He met her lips with his and there was an aggression in his kiss that completely swept her away. He tasted like beer, the same taste she had in her own mouth for the past hour. His face was clean-shaven, his bangs were hanging in his eyes and she reached up with both of her hands and pushed them back, tucking the strands of hair behind his ears. She wanted to see his eyes, his face, and more of him. Their kissing quickly escalated. His hands found her waist and then the hem of her shirt and he lifted it up over her head and off of her. He had his fingers on her white lace bra, the same one she had taken off for her husband tonight. He felt her nipples through the material and then tugged downward on each of her bra cups at the same time to reveal her breasts. He touched her now free and quickly responsive breast with both of his hands and brought his face near them and found his mouth on her nipples, one and then the other, as she arched her back for him and softly moaned. It had been so long for her. Her body was past the point of ready. She was beyond eager. She pulled his shirt off of him, quickly getting it over his head as she straddled him and smoothed her hands over his hairless chest. She could feel his erection through his jeans as he completely removed her bra now and threw it onto the floor in front of the sofa. She reached down for the button fly on his jeans and undid the first two buttons as he pulled off her shorts and slid his hand into the front of her

Timing

thong. His fingers found her and she was instantly moist. God help her. She could not resist. She could not stop what was about to happen. She got off of his lap and helped him remove his jeans and then his boxer-briefs. She immediately wanted to take him into her mouth, but he stopped her. For a moment she felt disappointed but that is when he hoarsely told her, "This is your night, pretty girl. Allow me..." And she did. He slipped off her thong as she knelt over him. He was flat on his back, lying on the leather sofa as she moved herself over his face. His mouth was warm and every inch of her body was reacting to his efforts to pleasure her. But it was her mind that stopped her.

She shut her eyes tightly, hoping to chase away the thoughts. *Keep feeling this Tash, keep going, God just let yourself go. You need this. You deserve this.* She looked at her wedding ring on her finger. A six-carat diamond symbolizing that she is a wife. Someone else's wife. She could feel his tongue enter her and then slip out again as he returned to teasing her clitoris. It hardened and throbbed and throbbed some more. She was close as she heard herself yell out, "Yes! Oh yes! God yes!" And the next moment she knew exactly what came over her. Guilt. She didn't finish. She couldn't. She wanted to so badly, more than Jack Williams would ever know, but she just couldn't do this. With him.

She got off of him and stood naked on the floor in front of him and said, "I can't. I can't do this." The tears stung in her eyes, but she willed them away as he stared at her, still not having moved from the sofa. What a beautiful man, almost a decade younger than her, with an amazing body which was so obviously still quite aroused. It was his eyes that she couldn't stop staring at though. They were full of concern. For her.

"I'm sorry," she said to him, in barely a whisper.

"It's okay..." he responded as he sat up on the couch and grabbed his jeans and slipped them on commando, leaving his boxer-briefs on the floor. And Tasha remained standing where she was, still completely naked, with an amazingly fit body for a woman of forty-five years old.

"*Okay* that I am cheating on my husband? Or *okay* that I just pulled away from what was probably going to be the best sex of my life?" Again, she had tears welling up in her eyes, but refused to set them free.

"Both, I guess," Jack said, handing her clothes to her as she slipped each piece on, standing right there in front of him as if they had been together for years and completely comfortable sharing their bodies. "You are hurting and you need to lean on someone. I am not going to tell you to walk away from your marriage, I sure as hell am not going to become a reason for you to do that. This

Timing

was the start of great sex tonight, not a relationship between us." Tasha was listening and suddenly wanting to feel angry at him. Was he using her? Was she using him? She knows he's too young for her, so she had no choice but to agree with him.

"I get it, I really do. I needed you to listen, and to help me unwind with a few drinks tonight and... to touch me. I am not looking to love you, Jack Williams. I already love my husband."

"He doesn't deserve you," Jack said, taking her by the hand and pulling her down to sit beside him. "You are a beautiful, sensual, sexy woman with a heart the size of Texas." Spoken like a true cowboy, Tasha thought as she remembered him wearing cowboy boots earlier tonight. "Pardon the cliché, but just be true to yourself and that alone will set you free from the torment you have carried around for too long."

Tasha was thinking of his advice, dwelling on his words that certainly made sense and had also touched her heart. "No one has ever cared about me the way you seem to, Jack. I think I could get used to your guidance in my life... you know, as a friend. A friend with an amazing body that I'm going to regret not relishing in, all the way, tonight." She smiled coyly at him and he laughed out loud.

Lori Bell

"You are one hell of a woman, don't let anyone make you feel otherwise...you hear?" And then he kissed her sweetly on the lips. It sort of felt like butter melting in her mouth as they parted and she said, "I have not had this much fun, or felt this free in such a very long time. Thank you."

"I'm glad to hear it, and I'm flattered to assist with bringing *Fun Tash* back to life," he was smiling widely at her as she stood up and walked across the room to find her sandals by the front door. "Oh, and do me a favor, before you go..." Tasha looked back at him, still sitting there bare-chested and wearing only jeans as she was about to walk out of the door with her hand already covering the doorknob. "As you drive out of here tonight, make sure you didn't wake any of the dead out there... you were awfully loud in here when I was trying to give you what I hope would have been the best orgasm of your life." He was teasing her, and she howled with laughter. God it felt good to laugh again. "Watch it, sexy boy...I just might be back to cross the finish line."

And then she closed the door behind her.

CHAPTER 5

Luckily the two beers she drank earlier tonight had already almost completely worn off. As she was driving, and nearly home, Tasha pulled her cell phone out of her handbag. She hadn't even taken that handbag out of her car tonight. Not at the cemetery. And not while she was inside of the house on the hill with Jack. When she checked the home screen on her iPhone, she immediately was alerted to having missed three calls from Harrison. One, was just thirty minutes ago. It was almost nine-thirty at night and she was sure he had been wondering and maybe even concerned about her and her whereabouts. *Welcome to my world*, she thought, and a part of her did feel guilty about what she had almost done with another man. But, she stopped herself from going there in her mind. Harrison had made her sick with worry and wonder more times than she could ever recall. It was his turn to feel that way. And he was going to have to make some serious changes, and a genuine effort to help save their marriage now.

Tasha never called him back, she just continued to drive home and got there about five minutes later. She pulled into the garage and saw Harrison's car already there as she parked alongside of it and pressed the remote to close the door on her side of the garage. Their house was now all closed up for the night and she wondered what it was going to be like being alone in there with Harrison again.

But it wasn't Harrison she saw first when she stepped up two steps from the garage, opened the door and entered the kitchen. It was Spence, with his arm in a sling. "Oh my God, honey! You're here. What happened?" At ten years old, Spence usually acted very mature for his age, but at this moment he started to cry and explained how he had been in the emergency room tonight, getting an X-ray of his pitching arm. *Oh dear God.* Tasha was as visibly upset as her son at this moment. She ran over to him and pulled him into her arms. She was standing, he was still seated at the table and he had wrapped one arm around her waist. *His good arm.* "Are you okay? I want to

Timing

know how this happened!"

"He fell wrong on his arm while jumping on the trampoline at the Carter's house tonight." Harrison answered her question as he walked into the kitchen, still wearing his gym clothes. His eyes bore into hers. She knew he was upset with her. She was upset with herself now that she knew her son had needed her and she was not there. But how was she going to explain why she was unreachable?

"And you took him to the ER?" Tasha asked, now wanting all of the details. And feeling so guilty for not being there.

"Yes, I got the call from Stacy Carter on my cell while I was at the gym. The ER doctor said it's just a sprain," Harrison explained and Spence interjected, "No baseball for two weeks until it heals." He looked like a child who had been punished, and Tasha reached for his hand to reassure him. "It's okay, it could have been so much worse. You could have broken it and missed out on the entire summer season. It will heal, we will get you some physical therapy if you need it so you can get back into pitching as soon as possible, as soon as you feel ready. Okay?" Spence nodded his head, thanked his mom, and told both of his parents that he just wanted to go to bed and fall asleep to forget about what happened for awhile.

Harrison purposely waited until he knew his son was asleep. And then he confronted his wife. She was fresh out of the shower, having washed off the feeling of Jack on her. She had to forget what she did. What happened tonight with her son was like a warning siren going off in her head. *Get it together Tasha Wheelan! You have a family who needs you for chrissakes!*

"I had to lie to our son tonight, I told him you were helping out a friend who was sick. I didn't want him to know I had no fucking clue where his mother was or why you were not answering your phone!" Tasha was staring at him, sitting up in bed with his burgundy satin pajama bottoms on and bare feet. "So where were you?"

Tasha suddenly felt superior to him. And what an exceptional feeling that is for her. She has always been the one to follow him. Stand behind him. Whatever he says goes. Well, not anymore. She is standing up to him now. Or more importantly, she is standing up for herself. And it is about damn time. "I *was* with a friend tonight. I left my cell phone in the car when I stopped at the cemetery to visit mom's grave. I bumped into a friend out there and we connected for awhile." That was one way to put getting naked with Jack Williams and coming incredibly close. Close to having sex with him.

Harrison was thinking his wife didn't have many friends, at least not close ones, but he didn't say it. He

Timing

could see a change in her tonight, again. And he liked it. He liked seeing Tasha with less makeup, and stepping away from playing dress up and putting up a facade for everyone. She seemed real to him again. He wanted to be angry at her tonight, and he was, until she came home. He was relieved to see her alright. Especially after what had happened, or not happened, in their bedroom earlier this evening. "Well you really should keep your cell phone with you and on, and check the damn thing for messages when you're away from our children." Tasha noticed this was the second time tonight that Harrison specified *our* son and *our* children. And she called him out.

"So are we sharing things now, Harrison?" she asked him as he looked confused and said, "What?" to her.

"You know, our son, our children... are you implying that we are in a marriage and do share things?" Tasha was downright bitchy with him and he was ready to play along.

"Of course we share things, you are my wife." He got up off of the bed and met her at the foot of the bed where she was sitting. He was still standing as he pulled her up, by her shoulders, onto her feet. She was momentarily taken aback by his hands on her. He was not manhandling her, but he did use his strength to stand her up.

In her bare feet, and he in his, she was considerably shorter than him. She wasn't intimidated or scared, but she was curious. "What do you want from me, Harry? I love you goddammit and you can't seem to decide if you even like me anymore. I deserve to know where we stand and what we are going to do about us. This isn't a marriage anymore!" Tasha realized she had raised her voice and she instantly toned it down, hoping she didn't wake her son. "I practically begged you for sex earlier tonight and you left me on my knees. Do you have any idea how that made me feel? You know how long it's been since we've touched each other." Tasha instantly thought of Jack's body's against hers and she pushed that thought out of her mind.

    She didn't have a chance to think further about anything else because Jack used some force to guide her down onto the bed and he immediately climbed on top of her. He never said a word and neither did she. He just kissed her hard and full on the mouth and she responded while his hands moved up her nightgown. She had not been wearing panties and he discovered that immediately. Her nightgown instantly came off and ended up on the floor. He pressed his mouth to hers, then he moved his tongue to her breasts until she could not take it anymore. She reached for the waistband of his pajama pants and pushed them down and off of him. He too was naked now and she touched him, teased him, and then it was his turn

Timing

to finish what Jack Williams had started earlier. She didn't cry out, in fear of waking up her son, but she did experience an amazing rush as Harrison helped her come repeatedly into his mouth. And then he pulled her off of the bed, onto her feet again, and turned her around and plunged deep inside of her. And then it was him who let out a moan of pleasure that could have woken up the dead.

Afterward, they both lay spent on their bed. Their bodies were no longer touching, but they did feel a connection to each other again. Even if it was brought on by angry sex. It was there and it was alive, and she was feeling hopeful. Her husband does still love her.

CHAPTER 6

Disappointed. That's how she felt and continued to feel day after day, night after night, throughout the following month because life pretty much resumed with very little communication from Harrison. But, discouraged is not how she is going to feel anymore. Tasha is a changed woman. She is taking what Jack Williams taught her, or more like what he had resurrected inside of her, and she is trying with everything she has to put her marriage back together. She has all of the puzzle pieces. Not a single one had been lost. Just misplaced. Maybe even buried. But it was not too late. Tasha believes she is just as much at fault for her marriage crumbling over the years. Money had

Timing

changed her. She never lost sight of trying to be a loving mother. With everything else and everyone else, however, she became superficial. Tasha even questioned if her daughter had been wrongly influenced by her. She knew she told Ari one too many times which clothes were acceptable and unacceptable to wear, how to style her hair, and even what to say to other people. Had she not allowed her daughter to become her own person? Maybe that is why she had gone off to college, back to New York, with very little interest in coming home for visits. It was springtime and Ari had not come home since Christmas, and she rarely ever called her parents. Tasha is the one who checks in with her. Still wanting to keep her distance from home, Ari had already signed up to take summer classes and continue living in the college dorm. So Tasha made plans to go back to New York to see her.

***

Tasha drove from Baltimore to New York City to spend the weekend with her daughter. She reserved a hotel room near the campus, but she wondered if maybe Ari would want to stay at the hotel with her all weekend. She would wait and see how receptive she is to her this time.

Lori Bell

It took just a little over three hours for Tasha to make the drive to New York City. She didn't mind the time alone to think on the long stretch of interstate roads. She thought about how happy Spence is to be back playing baseball and pitching again after his sprained arm had completely healed. He had a tournament scheduled for the weekend and Harrison will take him, alone. Again, Harrison always came through when anything pertained to his kids. *Why couldn't he be like that with me? I'm his wife for chrissakes,* she thought to herself, and felt a wave of sadness come over her. And then she reminded herself of her mission to make her marriage work. She had seen Jack Williams a few more times since the night the two of them shared a couple beers and a little too much of each other at his father's house on the hill. She helped him on the grounds on her most recent visit a few days ago, and then they shared food and conversation again. His father appeared to be doing better and had taken a drive into town, just to get out of the house, with a lady friend who picked him up in a convertible. Jack explained to Tasha how his mother and father divorced more than twenty years ago and his mother still lives in Texas, where Jack had also chosen to stay with his mother after the divorce. He told Tasha he has flip-flopped between living in Texas and Baltimore for the last ten years. He confessed to wanting to get to know his father better, especially now since he has been sick and needs him and so he recently moved back to Baltimore with indefinite plans to stay.

Timing

Tasha met his father once on the grounds when she walked up to the house to talk after she saw him sitting in a lawn chair in the front yard. He charmed her, just like his son had. They shared some small talk but nothing too personal, and Tasha wondered how Jack had explained her being on the grounds to his father. Jack's father is seventy years old, and he spoke proudly of the years he lived in Texas. While on that subject, he made a comment which Tasha didn't fully understand. He said *Jack is needed back in Texas and should go back there soon.* Tasha didn't ask him, or Jack, but she wondered if there is someone, a woman, back in Texas who once had his heart. Or broke it. Jack was quiet about his past, and he still had not told her how he makes a living. When Tasha asked him soon after they met, he just said he *gets by with very little*. And he called himself a *simple man*. That appeared to be so true. Tasha believed him to be an easy man to talk to, and love. Although she was not in love with him, Tasha certainly cared about him and needed him in her life. And she would be sad to see the day come if he would return to Texas again.

***

After Tasha checked into her room at the hotel, she texted Ari to let her know she had arrived. Ari seemed excited to have her mom in town as she texted back with a smiley face and asked her if she could pack an overnight bag and come to her hotel. Tasha was elated, told her absolutely and reminded her to bring a swimsuit because the hotel had both an indoor and outdoor pool. Tasha wondered if Ari just didn't want her to meet her friends on campus, but even if that were true she felt elated her daughter wanted to spend the weekend with her at the hotel. She missed her.

When Ari knocked on the hotel room door, Tasha was immediately up off of the bed she was lounging on and quickly swung open the door. Ari looked so grown up, so pretty and so college-like to Tasha. She had her long blonde hair twisted into a tight bun sitting straight up on top of her head, and she was wearing black sweat shorts and a neon pink tank top. She was showing some cleavage and Tasha reminded herself not to critique her daughter's choice in clothing or anything else the entire weekend. She is a young adult now. It wasn't Tasha though who immediately voiced an opinion about clothing. It was Ari, and she didn't hold back when she told her mother she looked *younger and hot and what the heck had she done with her wardrobe?* Tasha was wearing the cut-off jean shorts she had borrowed from Ari's closet before, a tight-fitting navy blue t-shirt and Sperry boat shoes to match.

"You like my new style, do ya?" Tasha asked her, pulling her into a tight hug and then closing the door to

Timing

the hotel room.

"Uh, yes, I can't believe you actually look like this... you're usually so June Clever," Ari said to her, still feeling her eyes wide from the change she is seeing in her mother. It wasn't just the clothing. There was more. Her mother had a fire in her eyes, and she seemed more...fun. Tasha laughed out loud at her daughter's comment. "I've never been a wallflower baby girl, but I've decided life is too damn short not to let my hair down, every day."

And that is exactly what the two of them did all weekend long. They lounged in the sun by the outdoor pool, shopped at their favorite stores in the city, and even took a drive by their old house in Greenville. Tasha, who was driving, had asked Ari if she wouldn't mind stopping by their former neighbor's house. But, when they did ring the doorbell at the house across the street from where they used to live, no one had been home at the time. Tasha missed her friend, Kelsey being close-by. The two of them used to help each other out with their kids, who were the exact same ages. Tasha especially did everything she could to be there for Kelsey when her husband had died unexpectedly in his early forties from a brain aneurysm. Tasha had so many wonderful memories of living in New York, and she missed it. Being in the city also made her miss the home design business she used to own. Life goes on, she thought, but she wondered if it had really gone on for her. It felt more like she has been spinning her wheels.

When they arrived back at the hotel on Sunday evening, it was time for Ari to gather her things and go back to the dorm and Tasha needed to get on the road to go back home. Before they said their goodbyes, Ari had something to say. "Mom...this has been the best time you and I have shared in what seems like forever. I don't know if I am growing up or what, but I think happiness looks good on you so whatever has changed or whatever you're doing, keep it up."

Tasha had tears in her eyes as she pulled Ari close and whispered in her ear, "Thank you, that means more to me than you will ever know. I love you, baby girl."

***

She was feeling rejuvenated from the wonderful weekend with her daughter when she pulled into a gas station to fill up her tank for the three-hour drive ahead of her. She paid by credit card outside at the pump, and then she decided to stop in at the coffee shop next door to get a mocha to keep her going during the drive. It was already seven o'clock and she knew it would be after ten before she made it home. She hadn't planned on staying so late, but the entire trip to visit her daughter was bliss and she didn't want to see it end. When she opened the glass door to enter the coffee shop, she saw a woman walking toward her, so to be polite she stepped back to hold the door for her. And that's when she looked directly at the tall, dark-haired woman, *with legs up to her neck,* as she liked to always say to her. What a gorgeous bombshell. So beautiful and fit and fabulous. She was looking at her neighbor, Kelsey.

"You have got to be kidding me, Kelsey!" Tasha nearly screamed out her name. It was so incredible to see her.

"What in the world are you doing here and why didn't you let me know you're back in town?" Kelsey asked immediately pulling her close as she too felt overjoyed to see Tasha again.

"I actually took a drive through the old neighborhood yesterday, with Ari, but you weren't home when we stopped," Tasha told her as she noticed Kelsey's eyes on her, and she knew what she was thinking. Tasha was wearing white denim cut-offs, she has been obsessed with cut-offs lately, and a black sleeveless button down linen blouse. She also had on a pair of comfortable black flip flops for the long drive.

When Kelsey expressed her disappointment for missing her visit, she invited Tasha to join her for a cup of coffee, right now. Kelsey had her own latte to-go in her hand and Tasha agreed it would be good to catch up for a little bit, before she drove home.

The two women were sitting across from each other at a table, privately tucked away in a corner. Kelsey told her she had recently gotten married again, and swore it would be the third and last time. Tasha was there for Kelsey when she lost her first husband, before they moved to Baltimore, and later she had heard a former lover came back into her life again and she had remarried. Her happiness unfortunately had been short-lived with her second husband, but now Kelsey Reiss looked happy and content with her life after all she had been through to get to this point. And that is exactly what Tasha told her she too is striving for. A chance to be happy again. Truly happy.

While living directly across the street for many years, Kelsey had no idea Tasha was unhappy in her marriage. She seemed to live a life fit for a queen, but Kelsey is wise enough to know sometimes what is seen on the outside is a pretense. Especially when there's pain on the inside.

"You look amazing, Tasha," Kelsey said to her, "I personally love the new, relaxed look. I don't know what brought on this change in you, but you should hang on to it." That was pretty much the same suggestion Ari had given her earlier.

Timing

Thirty minutes had passed too quickly and Tasha regretfully admitted she had to begin a long drive home as the sun was beginning to set. Before they parted ways, Kelsey wished Tasha the *best of luck with Harrison* and she gave her some advice that put wind in her sail. "Do what makes you happy, but make sure you feel it in your heart first. And remember, sometimes we have to take that first step, even when we can't see the whole staircase."

***

Mile after mile, the hours passed quickly for Tasha as she let the radio set her mood. Slow songs made her longing to feel loved again. Up tempo songs had her singing along and feeling empowered. Driving and thinking. Hoping. And then wishing on a falling star she saw descend right out of the dark sky in front of her.

She wouldn't tell anyone her wish, because then it wouldn't come true. She smiled to herself, wondering what Jack Williams is doing tonight.

CHAPTER 7

It was close to midnight when she made it home. After slipping off her flip flops by the door inside the kitchen, Tasha went directly upstairs carrying her overnight bag into her bedroom. The bed was still made, and Harrison was not in their room. She set her bag down in the armchair near the master bathroom and walked back out of the room. She passed by Spence's room, noticing again that his door had been pulled closed but she opened it to be sure he is asleep in his bed. Harrison's car was in the garage when she pulled in, so she knows he is home. He wouldn't leave their son home alone at night.

Timing

When Tasha was walking through the downstairs living room, it was completely dark and as she went to turn on a lamp beside the sectional, she saw him through the French doors. He was sitting outside on the patio, in the dark. Not a single light or candle burning. Just Harrison, lying back in a lounge chair and she could see the face on his watch glowing in the dark. She opened the door quietly, trying not to startle him if he had dozed off but he immediately looked over at her.

"Hi, I didn't know you were out here," she said, walking barefoot on the stamped concrete patio. "I'm assuming you saw my text that I got a late start on the road tonight." He hadn't replied to her message. Tasha noticed and empty glass on the patio table. Harrison occasionally drank scotch at night.

"Yeah I got it," he said, staring at her in the dark. "Spence was exhausted when we came home tonight, but he will be excited to tell you in the morning how we took second place in the tournament." Tasha could see Harrison smiling, so proudly, and she let out her enthusiasm when she cheered, "Oh that's wonderful! I'm sorry I missed it. I'm very proud of him, and I know you are, too."

Harrison nodded his head in agreement. "How was Ari? Did you two get along okay all weekend? He knows their daughter can be difficult, but she is never as harsh with him as she is with her mother. Mothers and daughters just bickered differently than fathers and daughters. The bar was set so much higher for bantering. Maybe women understood how much the other could take. Harrison had always held back with Ari, even when he was terribly upset with her, because he was afraid he would make her cry. Her tears, from the very first time he held her, always broke his heart.

"Yes, we had the most wonderful time together. She actually stayed with me at the hotel all weekend! Her idea!" Tasha was still on a high from the way she and Ari connected. She knew the change in her had so easily warmed Ari. It was time for Tasha to be real again, with everyone in her life. She now recognized how she had gotten lost along the way, and so caught up in having money, living in huge houses, driving luxurious cars, and wanting for nothing. Well, now, she wanted the one thing money cannot buy. Her husband.

"I'm glad to hear that," Harrison responded. "She texted me tonight and told me how nice it was to spend time with you. And many of the other moms at the games asked about you as well. I wish you could have been there to see our son. They had some tough competition this time, so it was amazing they placed second...but when Spence tries his best he always wins."

Timing

She wanted to say she will be there for the next game and she knows Spence understands Ari sometimes needs her too, but the only thing she could focus on was Harrison's last comment. "So tell me, Harry... if we try our best, will we win too?"

"I don't know," was all he said as he got up from his lounge chair on the patio and walked back into the house.

She stayed outside, wondering why she hadn't stopped him. Begged him to talk to her. To tell her what he's thinking. Does he want a divorce? Does he want her to go back to being who she had become the last decade of their marriage? Cold and heartless toward him. Unresponsive to his arms reaching out to her. Always dressed fit to kill with her hair and makeup just perfect. But everything was not perfect. Their life together reeked of imperfection. Their marriage has been on a downward spiral for a very long time. She knew that all too well now, but if this was entirely her fault why couldn't he forgive her and meet her halfway in this attempt to repair their relationship? Deep down, Tasha knew this had not been all about her. This was just as much about Harrison. And maybe even another woman.

***

It had been a few days since she was back there. Back to where she felt a strong pull to shift her life into reverse to be with her mother again. The sun was too hot and beating directly onto her face. She wore sunglasses to keep herself from squinting and to keep those wrinkles around her eyes at bay. Some women believed laugh lines and crow's feet added character. Tasha was not there yet. She still battled with the mirror each time she noticed Father Time had made another appearance on her body. She managed to take care of the loose flab underneath her upper arms. She had hired a trainer at the gym to specifically help her tone those. She had a pinch-sized roll under her navel once that she fought to flatten for six months. And the list went on. What she saw and fretted about were things no one else ever noticed. She often had a distorted view of herself, never feeling like she looked perfect enough. But she was working on that. She was getting better, greatly improving at just letting those things go. Today she had left the house, dressed casually again in short black chino shorts and a sleeveless lime green lycra top, and very little makeup. Only eyeliner and mascara. She had a natural, flawless skin tone and had finally realized there is no need to cover it up with makeup. The temperature nearly reached one hundred degrees and the heat index made it feel well over. So makeup or not, it would not have mattered because it all would have melted and ran off of her face anyway. She had sent a large drinking cooler of iced water with Spence when she dropped him off at baseball camp. She knew the coaches were cautious and always kept a good eye on the boys, extreme temperatures or not, but she still worried about her son and wanted to take good care of him. She had four hours before she had to pick him up and she left everything go at home. No plans for dinner, and maybe she would clean later. Wealthy or not, she never did hire a cleaning service for her house. There was just something about cleaning up after your own mess. Her mother had taught her that and she never lost sight of it. Her mother was her rock. And Tasha felt crushed knowing her time was cut short with her. Who knew? *That is what is completely bananas about life,* she thought to herself as she stood over her mother's grave again, *you just never fucking know.* She giggled to herself as she cursed in her mind. That always amused Jack because he said cursing *just didn't fit her.* She is *too much of a lady.*

Where is Jack anyway? She was wondering. "I know what you're thinking, mom..." Tasha smiled, "I do come here for you, to feel closer to you. Jack is my friend. I've never had a friend like this before. I can talk to him..."

"And get naked when the mood strikes!" She hadn't heard him walk up or drive up and she jumped when she heard his voice behind her. She felt her face flush and then she laughed out loud at his comment. "Hey, not in front of my mother!"

"How've you been pretty girl? You sure picked a hot one to come out here." Jack's hair was matted above his eyebrows and he had his long bangs tucked behind his ears. He was wearing another sleeveless shirt, this one burnt orange, and he had on cargo khaki shorts with those tan work boots. She had never seen him in shorts. His legs were sun kissed so he obviously wore shorts often. Tasha was staring because it was a different look for him. An even sexier one. If that were possible.

"I'm good, thank you," Tasha said, shielding her eyes from the sun because even with sunglasses on it was overpowering. "How are you?"

"Ready for a break from the heat. Care to join me?" *Care? Oh dear Lord. I think I care too much. I'm supposed to be fighting for my marriage, because I want to. I really want to. But I'm very much drawn to this man. As a friend,* Tasha reminded herself, and said, "Sure, why not."

Two iced teas and ten minutes later, the two of them were sitting outside under the covered patio in the backyard. A ceiling fan was on high above them and they were enjoying a break from the hot sun. Tasha didn't expect to go inside, knowing Jack still had work to do on the grounds, and his father is home. She waited on the patio while Jack poured the cold drinks. "How's your father doing?" Tasha asked him.

"He's doing well, probably taking his morning nap right now or else he'd be out here sniffing around you,"

Timing

Jack teased her and Tasha defended him. "Oh stop it. He's very charming. Like father, like son." She winked at him and he turned the attention to her. He always does.

"So how are things with Mr. Wheelan? Has he opened his eyes yet to what a lucky man he is?" The flirtation between the two of them is always there. It was meant to be all in good fun, but sometimes it became intense.

"A little better, actually, but still frustrating at times. I don't know how else to describe it. When I feel like I'm getting somewhere as I slowly chip away at the wall between us, he shuts me out again."

"Does he want a divorce?"

"I've never asked him that, so honestly I don't know. I'm not sure if I want to know, or if I'm ready for his answer. He acts like he just wants to co-exist in the same house, with our son, but sometimes I get mixed signals from him," Tasha explained.

"Mixed signals as in he wants sex from you, but he won't talk to you?" Jack bluntly asked her, and Tasha immediately thought of him as a girlfriend. Women talk about things like that, didn't they? This newfound friendship with this man, who is still very much a stranger to her in so many ways, is nothing short of amazing.

"Ha! You're prying about my sex life, Jack Williams. Better not go there."

"So you're not having sex with him?"

"Not meaningful sex," Tasha confessed.

"So when was the last time?"

Tasha hesitated before she said, "The night you and I came very close."

Jack actually giggled when he said, "Oh so he finished what I started?"

Tasha smiled, felt her face flush, and she said, "I'm really sorry if I came on to you that night, I'm going to blame it on the beer." The two of them had not talked about it again. Not until now, well over a month later. Tasha wondered if what he said that night was a cover up. Had he wanted more from her than just sex? Would it have been *meaningful* and would it have led to something more? *Oh for chrissakes,* she thought to herself, *we cannot possibly go there. We have a friendship. Not a relationship.*

"You don't have to be sorry. I'm not," Jack said, drinking the last of the iced tea in his tall glass, and tipping it back further to get some of the crushed ice in his mouth. "I enjoy your company out here. It would be a long summer without you."

Timing

"What happens at summer's end? Where are you headed then?" She wondered if his father would then be well enough to take the reins on the cemetery grounds again. And what, or who, will be waiting for Jack back in Texas when that happens.

"I think I had better get us a refill on the iced tea if I'm going to answer all of those questions, pretty girl. Be right back." When Jack walked away to refill both of their glasses, Tasha felt irked. Why did he just walk away from her? He just did the same thing that her husband does to her when she wants answers. Maybe it was time to practice making a man communicate. And she was going to start with Jack.

When he returned with their iced tea, he said a nurse had arrived to check on his father and give him a breathing treatment. His lungs were still not completely clear from pneumonia.

"Do you need to be in there with him? Tasha asked.

"No. I need to be out here with you. You want to know where I'm headed, well I wish I knew. I do have a home in Texas. And I also have a relationship that is in limbo there. This summer is my escape. Maybe I will get my head on straight and stop making mistakes."

"What kind of mistakes?" she asked.

"The same kind you're making. Sticking around just to make other people happy."

Tasha momentarily thought about what he said, before she spoke to him. "My family makes me happy. I don't want to leave them. They're my life. Does being away from the people you care about make you happy, Jack?" She wondered if he is in love with a woman back in Texas and why he didn't want to be with her anymore. Or maybe he does?

"I can't say I'm living the life here, but I am content. I just needed some time, some space from the pressures of real life and when my dad needed me, I didn't think twice. I do have to say though, I think I would be quite lonely out here if it weren't for you showing up." Jack smiled at her and Tasha agreed. She hadn't felt so connected to anyone in what felt like ages. She didn't want to depend on him always being there, but she couldn't imagine right now if he wasn't. She didn't even have his phone number but she knew she could always find him. Out at the cemetery. In an age where everyone freely swapped cell phone numbers, email addresses, and reached each other through various forms of social media, Tasha and Jack never went there. They just met on the outskirts of the city, on the cemetery grounds whenever their schedules collided. And it was Tasha who made a point here lately for that to happen.

Timing

"I agree, you've filled a void for me Jack. I'm not sure what we're doing here. I know we're building a friendship, and I also know we shouldn't be feeling some of the things we're feeling because we have other people in our lives depending on us. I'm sorry if I'm speaking for you, I just know what this would seem like to anyone on the outside looking in. I hope you know I depend on your listening ear, and I have fun with you. That's really it, I think, you're fun and I haven't had fun in a ridiculously long time."

"Tasha," Jack said to her, leaning closer to her. They both had their elbows up, resting on the glass tabletop in front of them. "I get it, I agree with you. And I don't care what other people think." And that was all he said before he pressed his lips to hers. She felt an instant tingly feeling all throughout her body that immediately intensified. His lips were wet from the tea and cold from the ice, and his tongue – she desperately wanted more of. And he gave it to her. They kissed deep and hungrily for minutes on end, until they were left breathless sitting outside under the covered patio of the house on the hill.

CHAPTER 8

A short time later, Tasha was back at her house and feeling terribly frazzled. The kissing, so consumed with mounting passion, did not go any farther. They talked at length about their connection and their growing attraction for each other before Tasha left. Jack didn't need any help on the grounds today, and Tasha thought it would be best if she left. Left before the two of them ended up naked in the grass. She kept thinking she shouldn't go back there. She was on the verge of cheating on her husband. Maybe she already was. They had not gone all the way, but Jack Williams definitely had sneaked his way into her mind, and maybe even into her heart. And now she believed he had come into her life for a reason.

Timing

Surprisingly, any and all thoughts of Jack escaped her because when she got home, Harrison was there. He rarely left the office early, only making exceptions for Spence's baseball schedule and he was still at camp so Tasha knew Harrison's surprise trip home in the middle of the day had nothing to do with their son. He changed out of his suit and tie and had on navy blue athletic shorts with a red baseball t-shirt that spelled out COACH on the back. He wore out that shirt while he coached a year of Ari's junior high softball. Harrison was standing in the garage as Tasha pulled her car in. She knew she had a surprised look on her face when she saw him and he responded to that.

"I guess you're wondering why I'm home, huh?" Harrison asked her as she got out of her car and closed the driver's side door.

"Is everything okay?" she asked, immediately feeling self conscious and hoping she didn't look like a disheveled woman who had just been making out. Her lips felt chapped and she was quick to take the back of her hand and wipe over them after licking off the taste of Jack Williams.

"Yes, I'm fine. I guess you've forgotten what today is..." Tasha had absolutely no idea what he meant. She and her husband never have plans together anymore so she was certainly baffled.

"Do you care to tell me what is going on? I don't have any reminders on my calendar today, and you never said anything to me last night or this morning." Tasha actually felt annoyed. He dictated so much of her life, she actually enjoyed her days when he was at work. Because, despite running a household, she did what she wanted to do with her days alone. Of course, today she is not proud of her actions but she will not allow herself to feel ashamed. She needs her newfound friendship with Jack.

"Happy Anniversary, Tasha Wheelan." When he said those words to her, her jaw dropped. She had forgotten all about it. She is the one who has remembered every year and felt like she always had to remind Harrison. Not that they ever celebrated anymore, not that he ever wined and dined her, but she always made sure he knew it was their day.

"Oh my gosh, I–"

"You forgot. Sort of unusual for you to forget and me to remember. Where have you been this morning? I've been home for an hour and lunch is almost ready." She did notice Harrison holding tools for grilling in his hand, which he must have just retrieved from a cabinet drawer under the sink in the garage.

"Lunch? Do you want to tell me what you did with my husband?" Harrison laughed at her, really laughed, in

Timing

the most sincere manner. Tasha was so thrown by him and his new attitude that she was speechless. But she still had to answer his question. She explained how she had just been out to her mother's grave as they walked through the house and outside again to the patio, where the grill was smoking. He thought she was spending entirely too much time at her mother's graveside. He saw it as unhealthy, but he didn't say anything to her. He once thought the world of his mother-in-law and missed her in their lives as well. Harrison told Tasha to sit down while he finishes getting lunch ready.

He set her plate in front of her with a fillet, a baked potato which he left plain because he knew his wife shied away from the extra calories of butter and sour cream, and he had fresh mixed greens on the side. She took one look at her plate, and of course thought it looked delicious but she felt more concerned at the moment about talking to her husband than eating. He set a glass of iced water in front of her plate and his, and then poured them each a glass of chardonnay.

"Harrison, really, what is all this?"

"It's our twentieth anniversary," he said. *Twenty years*, she thought. *Happy years? Not quite. Not all of them. Not by a long shot. But, is this a turnaround? Is this some sort of peace offering?* Tasha was skeptical and wanted answers but first she began to eat the surprise lunch her husband prepared.

"Did you even have time to go into work today? When did you buy all of this?" Tasha inquired as she relished eating the mouth-watering steak, grilled to leave some pink in the middle as she preferred, and then she took a swallow of wine. This just didn't seem real. Minus the expensive steaks, this is how life used to be with Harrison. Comfortable and happy while they enjoyed the simplest things together, like sharing a meal.

"I did go to the office, but I didn't get much done. I kept thinking about how I wanted to make this a special day for you, to pull off this lunch without you catching me in the middle of preparing it. I really didn't know if you would even be gone from the house today. I never ask you those things anymore."

Tasha felt as if he were tugging on her heart. His words touched her more than she could express. He is finally reaching out to her. "Thank you, Harry. Thank you so much for doing this for me, for us. Happy Anniversary." He smiled at her and touched her hand, "You too, honey." *My goodness, when was the last time he called me honey? When was the last time he did anything special for me like this? When was the last time I felt loved by him?*

***

Timing

"So what's your story, Wheelan?" Tasha asked him after they had eaten and she was working on finishing her second glass of wine. She was going to stop with that glass before she felt too loopy, because she still had to drive to the park this afternoon to pick up Spence. "Why the turnaround? You know I have been trying to reach you for well over a month now."

"That's why," he said to her. "You have been different. You are more like yourself again, like the woman I first fell in love with. You've caught my attention, I like what I see. Hell, I love what I see."

Oh my God, how long has it been since he told her that he loves her? She felt like crying, but she was just too damn happy. "Say it, Harry..." He moved his chair closer to hers, and he said the words she wanted to hear. Needed to hear. "I love you, Tash."

Before she responded, he kissed her. He kissed her so slowly, softly, and sweetly as a tear trickled down her cheek. And then she came to the quick realization how this is the second time today she has been kissed sitting outside on a patio. Her thoughts moved to Jack Williams and stayed there for the next half an hour. When her husband asked her to go upstairs, she told him they had some time yet before their son needed to come home, and he followed her inside the house. *He followed her.* Since when did he step back to allow her to lead the way? She felt empowered and she led the way again when she seductively pushed him back onto their bed and slid her hands underneath his shirt, squeezing his tight pecks and then roughly removing his shirt. She took his nipples between her teeth, she moved her body downward and took the rest of his clothes off. She was still wearing her shorts and her shirt when she knelt over him and slowly gave him a strip tease. She ended up riding him, repeatedly, as he reached for her breasts with his hands, then found them with his mouth. He found her clitoris with his thumb as she continued to move herself on him. He waited for her to climax and then he too let himself go. She had screamed out his name, Harry, over and over, and he moaned aloud with just as much pleasure. But what he didn't know is although she may have said *his* name, she was thinking of Jack. Jack's hands, Jack's mouth, Jack's body. She finally had her husband back in every way, body, mind, and soul, and now she wanted another man.

***

When Tasha tore herself away from lying naked in her husband's arms on their disheveled bedding, he watched her bend over to retrieve her clothes which were strewn all over the floor, and then she dressed herself in front of him in their bedroom. He was obviously getting excited again and she giggled, trying to push the thought

Timing

out of her mind of the night she also dressed herself in front of Jack.

Harrison kissed her goodbye when she said she would be back in ten minutes with their son. He tried to pull her back into their bed, but she insisted she had to get going. She didn't want to be late and cause Spence to worry. He finally gave in and slapped her on the behind as she walked away. As she was descending the stairway in their home, Harrison reached for his cell phone on the nightstand next to their bed. He checked for any text messages or missed calls, and then he clicked on the gallery of photographs saved in his iPhone. The most recent picture was one of his wife. It was Tasha looking hot and bothered as she was kissing another man this morning.

The private investigator Harrison hired did his job. He followed Tasha, found out where she was spending so much of her time lately, and with whom. Today he had stood in the tree line far behind the cemetery, near the house on the hill, and with his four-hundred-millimeter lens he captured Harrison's wife with a much younger man.

CHAPTER 9

So Harrison knew there was a reason for the sudden, sort of youthful and definitely carefree change in his wife. He's not sure what he suspected, the thought did cross his mind but to have proof of his wife indeed having an affair was an unbelievably difficult truth for him to accept. So he did what he does best. He took charge and he owned it. He wanted his marriage, he wanted his wife, and no man was going to take her away from him. Maybe this was a rude awakening for him. He felt jealous and angry, but he wasn't about to call out his wife for cheating. Because he had been doing the very same thing to her, for years.

Timing

He had short-term mistresses, he had one night stands. But, for him, it was just sex. He never developed any real feelings for any of those women, never fell in love. He believed Tasha has always honored her wedding vows, until now, and it scared him to think she could be in a relationship. A relationship which threatened his marriage and the hold he's always had on the only woman he's ever loved. And he did still love her.

***

Tasha was slipping into a new little cherry red dress. It was sleeveless and low cut just enough to look sexy but not slutty. She had the same thoughts when she tried on the dress at the boutique last week. The feel of the expensive material did not disappoint, but the mere fact that a size four had felt snug this time did. Tasha had too easily gotten away from her workout regime in the last month. This past week, however, knowing she needed to look and feel good in that red dress tonight, she hit the gym hard every day. She looked healthier with six extra pounds on her frame, but she refused to purchase the next dress size up. She was looking at herself in the full-length mirror in their bedroom, her hair in an up-do, her makeup flawless, her red dress hugged her body, and her black stilettos made her as tall as she wished she was in bare feet. Harrison, looking dapper in a traditional black tuxedo, whistled as he came up behind her, wrapped his arms around her waist and spoke softly in her ear. "You look incredible... why don't we just stay in tonight?"

She giggled and spun around to put her arms around his neck. "Thank you, Harry. We can save what's on your mind for when we come home." Their sex life had done a complete turnaround. Harrison could not keep his hands off of his wife, and Tasha was in disbelief. She responded to his advances every time, thoroughly enjoying the new, improved, and finally attentive Harrison again. She didn't think twice what may have brought on this change in him. Little did she know he suspected there was something behind the recent change in her and hired a private investigator to follow her, which led him to the revelation that his wife has been in the arms of another man. He then wanted her back. In every way. She is his wife and he planned to do everything in his power to keep her. What a way to wake up and realize what you've lost. And Harrison is a man who always wins.

***

The black-tie event was held in the heart of the City of Baltimore at the country club where the Wheelans are prominent members. It is an annual event honoring city officials, business owners, and only the richest of the rich were invited. There were mentions of sizeable donations

Timing

to the city throughout the year and a silent auction always took place to make incredible amounts of money on new cars, cruises, and smaller scale things like a one-year membership to the country club.

While Tasha and Harrison mingled among the wealthy, she noticed he never left her side. He has always left her alone periodically and often times at length at functions like this. Tonight, he was attentive to her, including her in the conversations, refilling her wine glass, and occasionally touching her back or brushing up against her. He seemed happy with her again, and she relished that feeling. But, she no longer lived for events like these. She used to dream of the day they would be on the guest list and plan weeks in advance for her hair, the perfect dress and heels, and schedule a mani-pedi and makeup appointments the morning of. Tonight, she couldn't have cared less. The people they have been surrounding themselves with are superficial, Tasha thought to herself as she scanned the event's attendees. And yes, she recognized how she too used to be the same. Not anymore. She no longer wanted to fit in here. She just wanted to enjoy being with her husband and hear the announcement of his law firm being one of the businesses which donated sizably to the city this year, because that will be a proud moment for him and his business partner, and then go home.

Lori Bell

The evening moved quickly and that moment was minutes away. Tasha and Harrison were seated at a round table with Harrison's law partner, John Thomas and his wife, Gabi and a few others whom she didn't personally know. Tasha rolled her eyes when the woman seated to the left of Gabi made mention of her trainer who was *phenomenal at assisting her with getting rid of the extra flab around her middle last year.* Tasha was well aware of the extra six pounds on her small frame, but she for once in her life brushed off a shallow comment directed at her from just another rich woman who is stuck on herself. Tasha was ashamed that she too used to act like that. Harrison immediately came to his wife's defense when he told the entire table how he thinks his wife *could not possibly look any more beautiful tonight.* His words choked her up as her smile for him lit up her entire face and shown in her eyes. He loved her again.

When the mayor took the microphone, the crowd applauded him and rose to their feet. And when the ballroom was again silent, the mayor spoke. He began to say how he needed to mention something not on the script tonight, to honor a man who met his maker. Tasha was not paying full attention, her thoughts were drifting as she heard the mayor describe a simple man with a bank account even the wealthiest in Baltimore could not match. And that man had died this past week, donating five million dollars back to the City of Baltimore. The applause

Timing

roared and then Tasha could not believe what she heard next. "Not bad for a gentleman who called himself the public cemetery groundskeeper and lived in a very modest house up on the hill known as the backdrop of the burial ground. So here's to you, Jackson Williams!" The mayor now had a cocktail glass in his hand and he raised it high, as did the crowd.

Tasha felt her face flush, her hands shake. She couldn't bring her wine glass to her mouth. And Harrison noticed. "Must have been some guy," he said to her, over the noise of the crowd. "Must have..." she replied, and then thought to herself, *yes he was*. Tasha had only one conversation with him, but he impressed her with a keen sense of humor and genuine kindness. She knew his name was Jackson, she knew his son is a junior and goes by Jack. She knew more about that man and his son than anyone else in the ballroom tonight. Or maybe not so much. She certainly was stunned to find out Jack is the son of a billionaire. No wonder he is able to drift and live day-to-day without a real job, Tasha thought, and she wished she had known. She wished he had told her more about himself and his life. And now she wanted to get to him. She wanted to run to him. My God, she had to offer her sincerest, deepest sympathy and be there for a man who has been there for her. It's only been several weeks, but their bond, their connection, means something to her. Tasha's thoughts were racing and when she turned toward her husband, she saw him watching her. She was startled for a moment but immediately calmed herself with the reassurance that there is no possible way Harrison could read her mind right now.

The rest of the evening's benefactors and chatter about each one fell on deaf ears. Tasha even missed the announcement of Harrison's law firm and their donation of one point five million dollars. He had nudged her then and she pretended to be in the moment with him. She was proud of him, but all she could wrap her head around is Jack and how he had just lost his father, days ago. And she had not known.

***

Hours later, she was lying awake beside her sleeping husband and her thoughts were consumed with Jack. All alone. In that house up on the hill. Maybe he was drinking a beer to lessen the pain and the sadness. Maybe he was making plans to move back to Texas. If only the weekend would pass quickly and she could get to him again.

CHAPTER 10

When Harrison left for work, Tasha also left the house with Spence. He had registered for a basketball camp at his grade school for the upcoming week. Before the season even began, Tasha mentioned to her son how she wanted to spend some quality time with him this summer and he had whined, wanting to attend all of the camps being offered so he could play sports and see his friends. Now Tasha was thankful for his plans because her first stop today must be the cemetery grounds.

She turned off of the highway and into the cemetery grounds and this time she passed up the road that led to her mother's grave. "Sorry mom," she spoke aloud, "I will be back to visit you later. I have to check on

Jack." Tasha continued to drive the path around the cemetery and up to the house on the hill. She saw Jack's truck parked in the driveway and immediately felt relief to know he is home this morning. She got out of her black BMW and walked up to the front door. There was no doorbell, so she knocked and waited.

When the door opened, he was standing before her in black gym shorts which ended just above his knees, no shirt and bare feet. His hair was a mess and the aroma of fresh coffee was coming from inside the house. "You slept in this morning," she said, feeling embarrassed for catching him like this.

"Yes I did, I had a late night last night," he said stepping back from the doorway. "Come in, pretty girl." As she entered the house, she removed her sandals by the door and Jack walked ahead of her and into the living room. He slipped on a t-shirt which was hanging over the back of the couch and she walked over to him. "I'm so sorry about your father, Jack. I had no idea, I thought he was getting better."

He smiled sweetly at her before he spoke. "I thought he was too, but his lungs never completely cleared and almost overnight the pneumonia came back with a vengeance. I've told you how stubborn he could be... he just waited too long or I should have kept a better eye on him. I don't know, you know what they say, it was his time." She held out both of her hands to him and he took two steps toward her and enveloped her into his arms. His shirt smelled like laundry detergent and his skin still felt warm from sleeping. She knew he hadn't been out of bed very long and just the image of him lying upstairs alone in one of the beds made her ache for him.

"Can I get you some coffee, I was just about to have some," he offered as they parted and she followed him into the kitchen. They both sat down at the old kitchen table, which Tasha thought seemed a bit rickety as she pulled out a chair from under it and sat down to hear it creak. Funny, she thought, how a billionaire had an old piece of furniture in his house. Maybe it was an antique. They both sipped the hot coffee, which Tasha said she drank black and Jack did too. And then he asked her how she knew his father had died. Tasha explained how she heard the announcement at the silent auction when the mayor spoke proudly of his father and beamed about the city's five million dollar donation.

"So now you know my father was loaded, and so am I. Bet you never would have guessed it seeing how he lived out here. And now you know I'm a simple man who doesn't have to worry about my next paycheck."

"No, I certainly would not ever have pegged you for having all of that money. You're the one who reminded me how to enjoy the little things in life, like a picnic under a shade tree or a beer on a Friday night. Jack, I'm so sorry you lost your father…and equally as sorry I was not there for you."

He reached across the table for her hand. "No need to apologize. You have a husband and a family to take care of. I am a big boy, I got this." But he was thinking how he could have used her to talk to the past several nights. He missed his father, he didn't want to be in this house alone. But, he and Tasha were new friends who met up once in awhile. He didn't even know how to reach her if he had to. He wanted her phone number, he wanted to see her more, but he knew better than she did that it was not a good idea to go there. Tasha intertwined her fingers with his. His hands were those of a man who had worked hard, not the hands of a man with money in the bank. His face looked so boyish this morning, even though he had overnight stubble on his face. And his eyes were sad.

"You may think *you got this* and it's okay to tell yourself that you do, but I know what it feels like to lose a parent you loved and needed and it's alright to let yourself grieve. Just be thankful you came back here this summer to spend so much time with him. That alone spoke volumes to him. He knew how much you loved him." As Tasha was speaking, she watched the tears well up in Jack's eyes and escape down his cheeks, and *thank you* is all he said to her before she stood up and wrapped

Timing

her arms around him. He kept sitting in his chair and he held on to her tightly as he buried his head into her chest and cried. He cried for the man he spent so much of his life apart from, but deeply loved.

After they finished their coffee and talked in detail about Jack's father and his wishes to be buried on the land where he lived, Jack excused himself to go get dressed and asked Tasha to wait for him. He had somewhere he wanted her to go with him.

***

The two of them walked behind Jack's father's house, almost all the way to the tree line, before Jack stopped. There was a concrete bench and a bird bath way out there, and Jack explained that is where his father enjoyed sitting, relaxing, and watching the birds. And then Tasha looked further to her left and that's when she saw the fresh ground, the mound of dirt, the simple wooden cross with no marker. "He's buried out here?" she asked Jack.

"Yes and he swore he wanted no extra fuss, no fancy stone, but I ordered one anyway. I want people to know, year after year, that Jackson Williams the second once lived, and was loved. He deserves a marker. Everyone does." Tasha moved closer to him and wrapped her arms around his waist.

Lori Bell

And that is the photograph which was sent to Harrison Wheelan's cell phone later in the day. The private investigator had panicked a bit when he saw them walking closer and closer to him, hidden in the tree line. He did not need a telephoto lens on his camera for this particular photograph of the two of them. He was just doing his job, but when he viewed the photograph on the digital screen on the back of his camera, he was proud of the money shot he had taken. You could definitely see in the photograph how much those two people cared for each other. Too bad for the woman's husband.

***

Her husband came home on time to eat dinner with her and Spence. Tasha had left the cemetery and Jack before lunch time. After she picked up her son from basketball camp, she tidied up the house and made spaghetti and meat sauce with a garden lettuce salad. Spence was in a talkative mood all throughout their meal, informing his parents about the fun he had at camp and the drills he learned. Harrison was listening intently and giving his opinion when Spence allowed him to get a word in edgewise. Tasha was watching them, loving their bond, and cherishing this time together. And little did she know her husband knew where she was today, and who she was with. She had not felt the least bit guilty for

Timing

running to Jack today. He needed her, and she was finally able to be there for him. When she left him today, they didn't make plans to see each other again. They just knew they would.

***

The three of them watched TV in the living room for most of the night. When Spence kept falling asleep on the couch, Tasha woke him and convinced him to go to bed since he had another early day for basketball camp in the morning. Once she made sure all of the doors were locked and the lights off, Tasha made her way upstairs. She thought Harrison seemed quiet tonight, and she mentioned that to him when they met up again in their bedroom. "I'm good, just tired, " he answered her as he slipped out of his pajama pants and into bed after letting them lay bunched up on the floor. Harrison preferred to sleep naked, he just hadn't for so many years because he and Tasha were not sharing any intimacy. In the past few weeks, he had returned to that habit and Tasha had most definitely noticed. When he got into bed, she went into the bathroom to moisturize her face and slip on her short white satin nightgown. She had already showered earlier in the evening, but had worn something more modest to lounge in downstairs with Spence present.

Lori Bell

While Harrison was lying on his back in bed, he stared up at the ceiling and thought of today's events. He was busy at the office, seeing clients every hour and then preparing for a court case tomorrow. He alerted the private investigator to how his wife may be headed out to the cemetery this week again. He knew this because he had seen how the news of Jackson Williams' death affected her. He thought to himself how any other man in this predicament would confront his wife and kick her out of the house and out of his life. He was not going to do that to her because he knew she refrained from doing it to him time and again, for so many years. He wanted to start over. He wanted a clean slate. He just did not know how to do that now, considering his wife has a boyfriend. He thought back to what happened today in his office right after he received the text along with another photograph of Tasha and that younger man. He felt raged. He felt pain. And that is when his secretary told him his barber was there to see him. Harrison is a busy man so he often made an appointment to have his hair cut at his office. Her name is Sarah Loft and she came to him again today. He looked up from his desk when she walked in. He watched her close and carefully lock the door behind her. He knew she was thinking he wanted more than just a haircut today, and when she began to unbutton her blouse for him he watched her. She was wearing a red bra and a black linen mini skirt that she started to lift up for him when she attempted to straddle his lap. He didn't put his

Timing

hands on her today. He just quietly told her he no longer needed her services, and asked her to leave. He stopped thinking about what he didn't want to do in his office today when his wife climbed into bed beside him and he reached out to hold her. He wanted forgiveness for all the times he betrayed her. He needed to forgive himself because he knew the guilt alone could kill him if he'd allow it. It is time to move forward. Now, he only wanted more than anything for his wife to forget that other man.

CHAPTER 11

Two weeks later, Tasha made her way through the dark in the middle of the night as she headed down the stairs in her bare feet and short pink satin nightgown. When she reached the living room, she turned on a Tiffany lamp her mother had given her many years ago. She couldn't sleep so she had gotten out of bed and decided to go downstairs for awhile.

She sat on one end of their sectional, with her legs crossed. She didn't want to recline or lie down. She didn't want to go into the kitchen for a glass of water, or something stronger. She had been thinking all night about how tomorrow will mark two and a half years since her mother was killed in that awful car accident.

Timing

Tasha can still remember where she was at the exact moment she got the call. The call came from the hospital. Mary Collins had always kept a small yellow post-it note in her purse which she laminated to withstand time. On it, she had written, *In case of an emergency, call my daughter, Tasha* and she had two phone numbers listed where Tasha could be reached. At home. And her cell phone. A nurse had reached Tasha her on her cell phone while she was driving to a morning hair appointment. *There's been an accident. The emergency personnel found your number in your mother's purse. Please come quickly...*

When Tasha arrived at the hospital, she was in pure panic mode. *If something happens to my mother, I do not know what I will do. Please tell me she is okay.* Mary Collins was not okay. She had died at the scene of the accident. The driver had crossed the center line and hit her head on. She had been driving a small, compact PT Cruiser and the other driver, a fully intoxicated man, was in a full-sized pick-up truck. Her mother suffered from head and neck injuries which instantly had taken her life, and the man who caused the accident walked away with only a few cuts and bruises, Tasha was told by the police. After the funeral, a police officer on the case came to Tasha's house and asked her if she wanted to press charges. She inquired about the other driver, and the officer told her what he knew. The man, in his early thirties, had a wife and two children. He was prepared to face the consequences of his actions. He didn't spend much time in jail because his family had bailed him out. He had nothing else on his record so Tasha decided he should not go to jail, especially when she learned the man had a family to take care of. She would give those children and wife the chance to remain together as a family. It was painful enough to know her family suffered the loss of a member. She wouldn't be the reason another family was torn apart. She is not a hateful person, and she wasn't hell-bent on seeing justice served. She just wanted to be left alone to grieve.

Harrison had thrown a complete conniption fit. He, *the best lawyer in the City of Baltimore, would make sure that man rotted in jail for the rest of his life.* Tasha said no. It was her choice and she chose to allow the man, who had caused an accident that killed her mother, to move on with his life. She didn't know if she was thinking clearly then, and she probably for sure was not, but to this day Tasha did not regret leaving the hate behind. Looking back though, Tasha knows she started to withdraw from herself and even more from her marriage from that moment on. No matter what Harrison said or did, to try to make her feel better, to try to reach her, it didn't work. Because she didn't allow him in. She chose to grieve alone, and after awhile, he left her alone.

Tasha was sitting in her dim-lit living room with eighteen-foot high ceilings and she laid her head back against the sofa and folded her arms across her chest. She still needed her mother, and she wondered if that emptiness would ever escape her. "I miss you, mom," she said aloud and then she heard a voice from the stairs. "She knows." It was Harrison. Tasha saw him standing there in his burgundy silk pajama bottoms, bare chest and bare feet as he walked toward her and sat down beside her. "And she's with you all of the time. You have to know there is so much of her in you. You are keeping her memory very much alive." He tried to say things like that to her right after her mother's death, but she never took his words to heart. This time she did. This time she felt the tears welling up her eyes as she looked over at her husband and took his hand in hers, and said, "Thank you."

"Do you want to talk about her? Or just tell me what's on your mind, why you're sitting down here all by yourself in the middle of the night?" Harrison asked her.

"For so long you never cared where I sat alone, or when," Tasha said to him and he never took his eyes off of her. "I thank God everyday now that I have you back and I want you to know if I had any part in creating the distance between us, I am sorry."

Harrison looked away from his wife. They were both to blame, and he wanted to move forward with her now and never look back. But he wondered if she felt the same way. He couldn't get the image out of his mind of his wife in the arms of another man. Would the day come when she asked him for a divorce and leave him? The ball seemed to be in her court now, and for the first time in his life Harrison felt powerless. "You don't have to apologize, Tash. We've both made mistakes."

Tasha was floored by his words. "What has gotten into you, Harry? I have never wanted out of our marriage, but I haven't always been happy in it either." She wanted to ask him now if he had ever been unfaithful to her, but she couldn't bring herself to say the words because she too had crossed the line. She may not have gone all the way with Jack Williams, but she could have. Easily. And she still thinks about him in *that* way.

And Harrison wanted to tell her he has not honored their wedding vows, he has had sex with other women. But he couldn't. He wondered if she already knew. He worried about the fallout from his actions if he were to admit what he's done. And, most of all, he feared losing her to the wealthy younger man who lived on the outskirts of the city behind the cemetery. "I want to change, I want us to make it. I've seen changes in you these past couple of months as you've found yourself again. I know our financial success went to both of our heads, I know we grew apart and never fought our way back to each other, and I know your mother's death sent you reeling. The change in you amazes me. I love how

Timing

carefree and fun you have become, and not to mention you are sexier than I've ever seen you. I'm telling you, those cut-offs you're so obsessed with lately pretty much guarantees an instant hard-on for me."

Tasha giggled. "Maybe I should go upstairs and slip on a pair?" she asked him and he touched her bare thigh. Her short nightgown was even shorter with her being seated on the sofa. "I want us to make it, too." she said feeling more certain than she has in a very long time. And then he kissed her, softly, slowly, and then more aggressively. They began to do entirely too much on the couch in the living room, with their son just one floor above them. While she still had her nightgown on, she whispered, "Let's take this party upstairs." But Harrison groaned, resisting her suggestion to stop. He didn't want to kill the moment. He wanted to make love to his wife right then, right there. He was overcome with the powerful feeling of *making love* compared to just having sex to satisfy the urge. He wanted to be a better man. Starting now.

Harrison headed up the stairs before Tasha, taking two steps at a time and she giggled at him as she bent down and started to turn off the lamp downstairs and that's when she heard a cell phone beep in the kitchen. She knew she had left her phone upstairs on the nightstand by her side of the bed, so she assumed Harrison had his phone charging overnight in the kitchen. She left the lamp on and walked into the kitchen, flipped on the light switch, and found Harrison's phone on the counter. She wondered if he had gotten a work-related text from his partner at the law firm or if there had been some sort of emergency with Ari. A text at one-thirty in the morning from anyone is unusual. She pressed the home screen button on Harrison's phone and what she read next sent shockwaves through her body. There were just two words sent from a woman named Sarah Loft who Tasha knew as Harrison's barber. A tall, shapely brunette, a twenty-six-year-old who had a barber degree and owned a popular shop downtown Baltimore. Tasha knew Harrison had gotten regular haircuts from her since they moved here almost three years ago. She had no idea Sarah Loft could have been one of those women. Not until she read the text meant for her husband. There were just two words in all capital letters typed in the bubble on the text screen. I'M PREGNANT.

 Tasha could not catch her breath. She bent over the counter top and tried to inhale through her nose. Her elbows were resting on the very end of the granite and she ran her fingers through her hair that had freely fallen into her face. She could feel the beads of sweat forming at her temples and on her forehead. *This is not happening. This is not happening. This is not happening.* Those words were repeatedly ringing in her ears as she fell to her knees and ended up on the floor with her back up against the cabinets. She had never found out for certain, because she didn't want to know if her husband had affairs. And now she had found proof in the worst possible way. He conceived a baby with another woman. He is going to be a father to more than just Ari and Spence. *Their* children.

She didn't move until Harrison interrupted the thoughts that were tormenting her as he rushed over to her on the floor when he entered the kitchen and spotted her. "What the hell happened? Are you okay?" He immediately knelt down before her and tried to reach for her hands. And that is when she threw his phone at him as hard as she could. It hit him on his bare collarbone, bounced off, and landed on the floor. His eyes were wide as he looked at her and went to pick up his phone which was now face down on the floor between them. "What is wrong?" As he asked her those words, he felt panicked. He knew someone had left him a message to make his wife look at him with the pain and rage he now saw in her eyes. "Everything, Harrison. Everything is wrong. Everything is ruined. And it's all because of you, you son-of-a-bitch!" She remained still, on the floor, as he turned his phone around and looked at the message. She watched the color drain from his face. She watched pure panic form in his eyes. He went from kneeling next to her to jumping to his feet. He took three, four, five, steps back and away from her. He threw the phone down on the table and held his head with both of his hands. He shook his head no, but he didn't speak. As she watched her husband, she almost felt sorry for him. He obviously was shocked and scared and hoping to stay in a state of disbelief. At least *there* he would not have to accept responsibility for his actions. His adulterous actions.

"Tash... I don't-"

"You don't know what to say? Well let me say it for you.... You have been screwing your hairdresser, and God only knows who else, and now this girl who is young enough to be your daughter is fucking pregnant. Congratulation daddy! Oh, and fuck you!" Tasha had raised her voice, but she prevented herself from screaming at him in their kitchen in fear of waking Spence.

"Stop, Tasha, please stop. You have to know I love you and my God we just found our way back to each other. I never meant to hurt you, I swear, it just happened. It didn't mean anything, it was just sex-"

"I don't care what it meant, you cheated on me! I guess it doesn't matter now, does it? That mere fact of you not being able to keep your dick in your pants has resulted in a pregnancy!" Tasha spat those words at him and she saw the tears that instantly sprung into his eyes.

"I can't do this," he said, and to her he sounded like

Timing

a little boy scared out of his mind. "I can't let this change everything for us. I won't!" Tasha watched Harrison gain strength from his own words as he rushed out of the kitchen and upstairs. She heard drawers opening and closing and a few minutes later he was back, fully dressed in faded, loose-fitting jeans, a black t-shirt, and his gray and red Asics that he wears to the gym. Tasha was still sitting on the floor. She didn't want to move because she didn't trust her legs to hold her. Her knees felt incredibly weak and her insides felt as if they were crumbling. This was a sickening feeling for her. This, she knew, was the end of their marriage. *How in the hell could they possibly salvage it now?*

He squatted down in front of her so he could be eye-level with her. "I know this is unbearable right now, but I am going to fix this. I will be back, and please, I am begging you, please be here." Tasha never said a word to him. She just looked away so he would not see the tears welling up in her eyes. He took her silence as a positive sign and he left before she could say anything to finalize what felt so much like the destruction of their life together.

And when he swiftly walked out the door, Tasha broke down for the first time in a very long time. She allowed herself to cry, and when she felt strong enough she said the words aloud and alone in her kitchen that she didn't want to believe were true. "You can't fix this, Harry."

CHAPTER 12

An hour and a half later, Tasha was upstairs in bed. She didn't expect to get any sleep as it was already three o'clock in the morning. She kept thinking about Harrison running out, going to *her*, he knows where *she* lives. He knows her body like he's only supposed to know his wife's. Another woman is carrying his child. Tasha wanted to stop her thoughts. *Just quit thinking about it*. But, this is real and she has to think about it and deal with it.

When Harrison walked into their bedroom minutes later, he saw her awake. He sat down on the cushioned armchair across the room, because he was scared to climb into bed with her. Fearful of what she is thinking and feeling about him now. Neither of them spoke for awhile and then Harrison did. "I know this is a nightmare...but can I ask you for one thing?"

"You have no right to ask me for anything," Tasha replied, feeling cold and heartless and wanting to fight those feelings with everything she had. She could not go back there with him, not again. She would walk away, divorce him before she ever co-existed bitterly with him again.

"I know I don't, but I need you to hear me. Please..."

"I want you to move out. I'm not leaving here, I'm not uprooting Spence. You need to be the one to go." As she said those words, she could have just bawled. That is not what she wanted. She didn't want to end their marriage, but considering the news which just rocked her to her core in the middle of the night, she felt as if she had no other choice. She rode her husband's coattail for many years, and now she finally felt done with playing follow the leader with him. She is stronger than that. She deserved better than Harrison Wheelan.

Timing

"No," he shook his head side to side, repeatedly as if somehow he could shake the words out of his ears that he had just heard his wife say to him. "We can get through this. I'm telling you, we can."

"And I'm telling you, I'm done." Tasha remained in their bed and Harrison stayed seated in the chair across the room. He bent forward, placing his face in his hands, and Tasha watched him while wondering how he had allowed them to get to this point. He has gotten another woman pregnant. She wasn't going to allow her mind to go there, but she wanted to know. What had he said to her tonight? What did she have to say to him? Does Sarah Loft, the barber, want a life with *her* husband? What if he didn't want her? What if he didn't want the baby? Tasha couldn't imagine Harrison turning his back on his baby, his own flesh and blood. He may be a man who has failed at being a husband, but he soared at being a father. He loves Ari and Spence and they adore him. Tasha worried about her children now. How were they going to react to their father's betrayal?

"I told her I do not want the baby," Harrison blurted out, and Tasha's eyes widened and her jaw dropped. "You what?"

"I do not want this child... it was not conceived in love. I bent her over my desk and fucked her. That is all it was."

"Oh my God, Harrison!" The visual that instantly flashed into her mind pained her. *Jesus. I can't go there.*

"You need to hear this. I do not even like her. I was attracted to her for sex. I sure as hell do not want to spend the rest of my life connected to her because of some child."

"*Some child* will have your blood, your eyes, your stance maybe. Can you really turn your back on that?" Tasha actually held her breath while she waited for his answer.

"I don't know if she's keeping the baby. There is a small window of time left yet for her to decide. I told her how I feel. She's not asking me for anything. She just wanted me to know that I could be the father of her baby."

"Could be? You mean she isn't sure who the father is?" Tasha immediately thought *what a whore* but momentarily felt relieved knowing Harrison is not the only possible candidate for fathering this unborn baby.

"I told you, I was not in a relationship with her so yes there could be a chance that I'm off the hook."

"Off the hook? Do you even hear yourself? You sound like you're trying to get out of working the concession stand at one of Spence's baseball games. This is a life we are talking about and now all of our lives are in limbo as we wait to see if your whore is carrying your

Timing

baby!"

"If she decides to keep it, we will get a DNA test done now, while she is pregnant. We are not waiting." Harrison had demanded the test be done and insisted on paying for it to ensure she will do it now and not seven months later. Sarah Loft is already two months along.

"So, what I think I'm hearing is you want me to sit tight while we wait and see if you have a baby on the way? You're thinking we can just move past this and live happily ever after. It doesn't work that way Harrison, you cheated on me. Do you have any idea what that feels like?" As she said those words she only thought of how she is feeling. It never in a million years would have ever occurred to her that her husband had her followed and it both crushed him and encouraged him to fight like hell for her when he saw those pictures of her in the arms of another man.

"Tash..." He stood up from sitting in the chair and pulled his cell phone out of his pocket. He walked over to her and sat on the bed in front of her. "I do know what it feels like. I've never in my life felt anything so crushing." He turned his phone to her and she was utterly shocked to see a picture of her and Jack Williams engulfed in a passionate kiss. He knew. He knew and he had not confronted her. He knew just like she thought she knew, time and again, that he was having an affair. She thought back to herself reversing her car out of that parking spot at The Sierra hotel and deciding not to catch him in the act.

"I... You had me followed?" she asked, feeling like he had so suddenly turned the tables on her. She never slept with Jack, but she had come damn close that one night.

"The sudden change in you caught my attention. I had to know, so yes I hired a private investigator to see where you were spending your days. Look, Tasha, I am not asking you for an explanation. I'm not even asking you to forgive me, not yet. I just want you to understand... and I think you already do."

He was using this against her. And maybe he had every right to, but Tasha felt herself teetering again between feeling strong and caving. "No, I don't," she said, surprising herself. "I never had sex with him. He became my friend, a confidant, but I couldn't go all the way. I wanted to... it had been so long since you touched me. My body was craving a man, but my mind stopped me because it was wrong. You can't say the same, can you? I know the barber bitch was not your only affair. It's been years since we had a real marriage and intimacy. Don't lie to me anymore, Harrison. Put all of your dirty cards on the table." Tasha had no idea where this strength suddenly came from. Maybe a small part of her did *understand*. And, if so, she had Jack Williams to thank for that. But understanding did not mean she is on the road to forgiveness. It wasn't that easy.

"You didn't have sex with him? Well it sure looks like the two of you were doing more than playing checkers together. He had his hands on you, his mouth on you, and the idea of him or any other man seeing you, all of you, and being with you like that simply kills me. Sex was just sex to me for so long, until I saw you in these pictures," he said, showing her the second picture of her in Jack's arms while standing at his father's grave. "It hit me when I saw this. That is when I was done with other women. I came back to you, body and soul, as I want to believe you have to me. Are you still seeing him?"

"As a friend who is there for me when I need to talk to someone," Tasha attempted to explain.

"Okay," he said, not knowing what else to say to her. He wanted to demand she cut all ties with him, but he knew he couldn't. Not now, because that would only make her flee to him.

"I'm not having an affair. You can call off your watchman." Tasha felt like she held all of the cards and she again liked this feeling of power. It made her feel strong and it has taken her a long time to realize her own strength.

"I don't need to see anymore pictures. I believe you when you say this is some kind of a friendship, but I'm scared... scared that you will run to him now that I've made such a mess of things." Harrison's sincere words, his honesty, touched her.

"I don't know where to run, who to turn to anymore," she said, still reeling from the baby news. "I just know we need some space between us now. We need to see how this mess plays out. And you need to take responsibility for your actions. Your barber may not be someone you *like* but she is a woman who could be carrying your child so that makes you connected to her. At least for a little while, until you have all of the facts."

"I would do anything to reverse this pain I'm causing you, Tash," Harrison said as he reached for her hand. And she immediately pulled away from him.

"Then pray this baby isn't yours," she said moving her body over to the opposite side of their bed from where he was sitting beside her, and when she turned her back to him she felt a tear trickle off of her cheek and melt on the pillow.

CHAPTER 13

The next few days crept by as Tasha and Harrison remained in the same house, sharing small talk in front of their son who had instantly recognized the tension between them but when he asked his mom about it, this time she acted like nothing is wrong. She mentioned how *sometimes couples go through rough patches but everything will be just fine.* Spence was worried but he believed his mom when she reassured him. The timing of Tasha's reassurance was pertinent because her son was all packed up and ready for four days of summer camp. He was looking forward to staying in a cabin in the woods with all of his friends and taking part in outdoor activities, day and night. Tasha knew she would miss him, but she was relieved to be able to stop pretending around Harrison for a few days. They had not talked about Sarah Loft's pregnancy since the night she sent the text and shocked them both. They were not sharing a bed either. Tasha had waited until Spence fell asleep the past few nights before she went into Ari's room and slept in her bed. She didn't want to be near her husband. She hated the mess he caused, and even more she hated the limbo their lives are in now. The state of not knowing if the baby is his has brought her some hope, hope that her marriage could be saved and their lives will not be forever changed. And she hated feeling that way. She should not still want him after this pain he has caused her. But she did.

After she brought her son to the bus stop for the camping trip, Tasha drove directly to the cemetery. She had not seen Jack since the day she stopped by his house to offer her condolences after his father passed away. She thought of him often and especially missed him the past few days when she needed someone to confide in. Today she was hoping he would be around for her to talk to.

Again she passed up the turn that led to her mother's tombstone and drove directly up to the house. Jack's truck was not in the drive. She parked her car anyway and walked up to the door. She knocked but he never answered. She wasn't ready to go home so she walked around to the back of the house and sat down in a chair on the patio. She sat there thinking about her life and trying to figure out exactly who she is. And what she really wants. For so many years she has been Harrison

Timing

Wheelan's wife. A mother to Ari and Spence. She relished in the success she had with her own home design business when they lived in New York City. She remembers the feeling of self worth which she obtained from that success. Maybe it was time for her to dive back into the business world. She felt on the verge of having to make so many decisions. Life-altering decisions. Should she walk away? Could she actually do it? Or should she try harder, fight for what is hers and has always been hers?

Tasha was deep in thought, feeling a warm breeze on her face as she sat on a patio that isn't even hers. But something about being there made her feel safe. She was wearing white Bermuda shorts with a sleeveless denim button-down shirt and dark brown ankle-wrap wedge sandals. She sat with her legs crossed, staring out at the open land and then her eyes reached the tree line and she remembered Harrison showing her the pictures of her and Jack out there. She knew from the angle of both photographs that the man hired to spy on them must have been hiding in the trees. She wondered if he is there again today, and before she could sink any further into her thoughts, she heard a voice behind her as Jack opened the patio door from inside of the house and stepped out onto the concrete. He was again wearing his work jeans and a sleeveless white shirt and his feet were bare. She smiled to herself, knowing his father insisted on no shoes in the house to keep the floors clean, and Jack was still honoring his request even after he was gone. "Well this is a nice surprise," Jack said pulling up a chair beside her, and she was looking at his feet. Some men had sexy feet and this man did, she was thinking to herself as she smiled at him and spoke. "I didn't know where else to go," she grew serious again, "and it seems like if I want to find peace, I can do that here."

"Well I'm glad you feel the way you do, like you can come here. I wish I felt that pull to somewhere in my life," Jack said, feeling happier than he has in awhile having her there with him again. He really missed her lately. Almost as much as he missed his father. He was sick and tired of missing people in his life. The house on the hill had become a very lonely place for him.

"You're missing your father, and you're feeling angry and lost," Tasha said remembering how she felt when her mother left this earth. "Those are all very normal feelings that I can't say will eventually pass, but you will get used to the fact that he's never coming back and finally you just accept it because you have to."

"Spoken like someone who has been there," Jack said to her, sitting up in his chair so he could be closer to her. "Can I get you a drink or something?"

"Yes, a beer." She kept a straight face as she

Timing

watched Jack break into a smile and chuckle out loud.

"Oh no, pretty girl, we both know it doesn't take but one or two and your clothes are falling off."

"Maybe that's what I need," she said to him, still appearing so serious. "Maybe I need to get drunk and forget it all and do something without a conscience for once."

"Tell me what is going on, Tasha. You obviously need to talk, and I'm your man." As he said those words to her, she wondered if maybe he is. Maybe it is written in the stars for her to rob the fucking cradle and spend the rest of her life with this man. For now, she wouldn't get too crazy with that notion and she would just take advantage of his listening ear.

"My husband may have gotten his barber whore pregnant, DNA results pending." That almost sounded comical, but Tasha didn't feel like laughing. "And apparently my husband isn't the only possible father."

"Are you serious? Oh shit, how awful." Jack shook his head and reached for her hand. "I think you do need that beer."

He never went inside to get her a beer, but he did sit in silence as Tasha explained how they are still living in the same house but separately. She told him how they had reconciled and truly began to move forward in their marriage, in their life together. And then this bomb was dropped on them. This bomb that Harrison created through his adulterous actions. And it will be a ticking time bomb until the test results reveal whether or not Harrison is going to become a daddy. Again. Only this time, not with her.

"I feel like this should be the last straw, I shouldn't want him anymore. But what am I doing? I'm hoping this baby is not his. I'm hoping there is still a chance to salvage our family. I'd like to think I'm doing this for my children, for the family I want to stay together, but I know I'm doing it for me. I don't know if I am strong enough to walk away and make a life on my own. I guess I don't deal well with change. Or call me a coward."

"You're hardly a coward, and you should know that picking up the pieces takes more courage than walking away." Jack's words struck her.

"What have you walked away from, Jack Williams?"

"This is about you today, pretty girl," he said, "I'll save my story for another day, if you promise to come back."

"Only if you chase away any unwanted photographers in the tree line," Tasha said to him, and

Timing

then explained the private investigator who Harrison hired to take photographs of them. Jack immediately went inside to put on his boots and the two of them took a walk through the backyard and into the trees. There was no one else around and no cars were driving off in the distance on the back roads. "Looks like we're alone out here today," Jack said pulling her close. He was only a few inches taller than her in her wedges and he met his lips with hers. She kissed him back, long and slow. He was holding her face in his hands and she had her arms around the tight muscles in his torso. It felt good to be with him, to kiss him. No matter how incredibly wrong she knew it was.

***

As they were walking back to the house still touching and stealing intense kisses, their passion was mounting. Tasha knew what she was about to do could be something she will regret for the rest of her life. But she was going to do it anyway. Her anger toward Harrison had completely surfaced and maybe she just wanted to get even. She had been contemplating forgiving him if this baby turns out to not be his. She had also thought about leaving him, walking away from him forever. She was just so sick and tired of being indecisive. *Give up. Try harder. Have the guts to make a decision!* It was time she lived in the moment. And that is exactly what she is about to do.

When they reached the back of the house, he slid open the patio door and stepped back for her to enter first. He was touching her bottom as she stepped up the concrete step and into the house. She was giggling as she felt his hands reach up inside of the front of her shirt. *Jesus she could hardly wait any longer. She wanted this man.* And then a hard, almost frantic, knock on the front door stopped both of them from going up the stairs to his bedroom. He looked at her, said he was *not expecting anyone, but hold on a second.*

Tasha watched him walk toward the door and he opened it to find a woman, who looked to be in her early thirties. Standing an inch or so taller than Jack, she had poker-straight dark hair hanging down to the middle of her back. She was wearing tight white jeans and a black tank top. Her skin looked fair and her eyes were fixed on Jack. "Brooklyn...what are you doing here?" Tasha, still standing about ten or fifteen feet behind Jack and in front of the stairs leading to the upper level of the house, felt awkward. But not half as awkward as she felt when two little girls, around the ages of four and six, came up running from behind the woman at the door and bounced into the house and sprung into Jack's arms. He immediately squatted down on the floor and enveloped them both into his big, strong arms. And that is when Tasha heard those little girls call him *daddy*. Amid the squeals and the hugs and kisses, Jack managed to stand

Timing

up while holding both of the little girls. *His* little girls.

The woman closed the front door behind her and then finally made eye contact with Tasha. Jack saw how awkward Tasha felt, he was feeling it too. Probably even more so.

"I'm Tasha, I was a friend of Jackson Senior and I just stopped by to offer my condolences to Jack." Jack was watching her, thinking how she didn't have to fabricate a story, but he appreciated her for being respectful in front of the girls.

"This is Brooklyn, and these two are Ava and Lily." Jack said as the little girls held tight to him and Tasha managed to say hello, calling them both by name as she stepped closer to the doorway. She needed to get out of there. And quickly.

"I'm Jack's wife," the woman named Brooklyn said, rather abruptly, as if she were making a point to let both Tasha and Jack know how she was on to them. It was as if she could see right through their frontage. Maybe she knew they were headed upstairs and about to become lovers. Tasha knew her last thought was probably far-fetched, but she also felt like the impossible had just occurred. Jack Williams is a family man. She had so many questions as her mind was reeling, but it was time for her to leave. She felt like the odd woman out, and she deserved to. But it was Jack's fault for keeping the truth from her. He has been living in Maryland, completely on the other side of the country from his family. What kind of man does that?

"It's nice to meet you all, but I do have to get going," Tasha said passing them, reaching for the front door and then she looked back at him as he spoke to her.

"Thank you for coming, I know how much you cared about him." That is all Jack said to her, and just as he had hoped she would, she read between the lines. He was not talking about his father. He was talking about himself. Jack knows how much she cares about him, and he hoped Tasha knew he reciprocates those feelings for her. She certainly does know, and this revelation was all the more painful because of it.

***

Tasha was driving and on the verge of crying as she exited the cemetery grounds. *Lord have mercy a few minutes later and that woman and her children would have walked in on us in the heat of passion. Jack has a family. He has a fucking family. What am I doing with him? I really don't even know him. Obviously.*

She knew what she had to do. She must forget this fantasyland she has been caught up in with Jack Williams.

Timing

She is not going to break up a family. She would be no better than the barber whore who did more to her husband than trim and clip him. If Sarah Loft is pregnant with Harrison's child, she will be partly responsible for breaking up their family. Tasha didn't know what she wanted or expected from Jack, but believing anything at all is possible at this point is now out of the question. She did, however, know what she wanted from her own husband and she was on her way now to Harrison's office.

CHAPTER 14

She parked her car in the parking lot of Harrison's law firm. As she sat there, she pulled the visor down in front of her and looked in the small rectangular mirror. Her hair was windblown, her face looked rosy and she knew she smelled of the outdoors. She had only stopped by Harrison's office a handful of times since they moved to Baltimore and she knew for certain all of those times she had been dressed to the nines. She didn't even miss donning the dresses and heels now, but at this moment she felt a little self conscious in shorts and sandals. She decided seeing Harrison right now is far more important than how she feels being dressed down.

Timing

After she ran her fingers through her hair and applied a fresh coat of lipstick and then eyeliner, she entered the building and took the glass elevator up to the third floor. When she reached Harrison's secretary, she smiled. "Mrs. Wheelan? Hello, my goodness it's been a long time. How are you? You look great!"

Tasha immediately felt better. There is just something about a compliment from one woman to another that will boost self confidence. "Thank you, Jenna. I didn't plan to stop in here today so please excuse how I'm dressed."

"No need to, I wish I could slip into comfy clothes today and be anywhere but here, but shhh," she put a finger to her lips, "don't tell your husband I said that because he thinks I love my job." Both women giggled and then Tasha asked if Harrison is in his office.

"I just got back from running an errand and I believe he is in there without a client," Jenna told her. "Would you like me to check first?"

"No, I'll take my chances," Tasha said, walking toward his office door as Jenna picked up the ringing phone on her desk and waved at her as she answered it.

Tasha knocked once and opened the office door. She expected to find him sitting behind his laptop with his reading glasses low on his nose, or maybe even pacing in front of the window that took up an entire wall in his office while he spoke to a client on speaker phone. Instead, she saw Harrison standing in front of that window, staring out of it while a woman sat in one of the two chairs parked in front of his large desk. She had been talking to him and he appeared to be listening without giving her any eye contact. Tasha immediately recognized her. She had stopped talking and stood up from her chair as Tasha came in and closed the door behind her. Harrison's eyes were wide as he kept his arms folded across his chest and turned his body away from the window and toward his wife.

"I didn't expect to find *her* in here," Tasha said only looking at her husband. "But, then again, you've apparently paid my husband quite a few private visits haven't you?" Tasha moved her eyes over to Sarah Loft. She didn't look pregnant, and she really didn't look like a whore. She was wearing a black pencil skirt, black pointed-toe heels, and a peach blouse with three quarter length sleeves, untucked and very low-cut. Tasha could see entirely too much of her cleavage and recanted her own thought. She did look like a whore. Sarah Loft glanced at Harrison as if he was supposed to say something in her defense. He didn't dare. He was flabbergasted at the way Tasha had been holding her own for months now. She wasn't the woman who expected him to always take the wheel. He had control for many years.

Timing

Tasha knew how to spend money and raise children, but everything else she left up to Harrison. She followed his lead. Not anymore. She says what she is thinking and she is bolder...and more beautiful than ever to him. "She was just leaving," Harrison said, obviously giving Sarah Loft the cue to get the hell out of there.

"Oh no, do not leave on my account. Carry on. I'd like to hear the latest with this soap opera, especially since it has greatly impacted my life." Tasha's eyes were stinging. *What kind of a woman sleeps with a married man?* And then she immediately caught herself. *A woman like her.* She had almost given in to her desires with Jack Williams. And now she discovered he is a married man, with children. Tasha realized she did not know Sarah Loft and as badly as she wanted to judge her, she needed to stop. She just wanted to get her out of their lives. If the baby she is carrying is Harrison's, that will never happen unless Tasha walked away first. And she didn't know if she was ready to do that.

"Mrs. Wheelan," Sarah Loft spoke with a shaky voice, and Tasha continued to look at her despite the fact that she was feeling old being called *Mrs.* by a woman nearly twenty years younger than her who had slept with her husband. "I could say I'm sorry, but I'm not sorry." Tasha glared at her and Harrison looked as if he was about to step in and escort her out the door. "What I mean is...I was told I would never have children. This pregnancy is a miracle." Tasha did all she could not to roll her eyes. Maybe it was Sara Loft's miracle, but it was her nightmare. "I came here today to tell your husband I am keeping my baby. And I also refuse to do anything to jeopardize the health of my baby while I'm still carrying him or her. I will not be having a DNA test done until after my baby is born."

Tasha's eyes widened as she looked over at Harrison. They were going to have to wait several months, depending on how far along the pregnancy is, to know the truth. "We have a right to know," Tasha interrupted her.

"And I have a right, as this baby's mother, to make the final decision as to when this test will be done. And it will be after my baby is born. And if you've noticed, Mrs. Wheelan, I have said *my* baby repeatedly. I don't care who the father is, this baby is mine. So if you want to go on with your life, please do. I don't want your husband. I never did."

"You are a fucking whore!" Tasha spat those words at her and Harrison swiftly walked toward her. He knew better than to say anything to her. He just stood close, in case Tasha would try to physically tear Sarah Loft apart. Again, his wife's boldness amazed him.

"Yes I know, and I'm not too proud of that right

Timing

now." And that was all she said as she picked up her handbag off of the chair beside her and walked out of the room. She left Harrison and Tasha standing there in silence. He was wondering why she had stopped by, so he asked her. "Do you want to tell me what brings you here today? I don't know the last time you came here..."

Tasha ignored his question. "Do we seriously have to wait nine months to find out if that woman, who you screwed right here in this office, is carrying your baby?" Tasha walked around the room and ended up behind his desk. "So this is where you dropped your pants, huh? Was the fuck worth it, Harry? Was it worth this insane mess you are in now? She is trouble, and God help you if you have to raise a child with her."

Harrison sighed, feeling remorseful, ashamed, and downright sick to his stomach. His list of regrets had reached its peak. If only he could take back the time in his life when he thought a cheap thrill never hurt anyone. "I'm incredibly sorry, Tash."

"I know you are," she said to him.

"So where do we go from here then?" he asked her.

"You are a successful, powerful attorney, make her have the damn test done!"

"I've already checked into it, she has the power on

this one. A mother's rights go a long way." Harrison sounded both frustrated and disappointed, but a small part of him felt hopeful. His wife could have walked out on him by now. She still could. But she hasn't yet. "You never did answer my question. Why are you here?"

Tasha walked around his desk and over to where he was standing in the middle of the room. "I am not the same woman you married. For the first time in my life, I can honestly say that I've found myself. I am forty-five years old and I finally know who I am."

"I know, and I'm very proud of you for that. You've really shown me what it's about lately. Laughing and living, really living, with you again has brought me to a place I thought I'd never get back to again. I love you, Tash. I need you. Please hold on, with me, to what we have."

"And if that baby turns out to be yours? What then? How will a baby you share with another woman fit into our lives? What are you teaching our children if that happens?"

"I don't know," he sighed. "I wish I knew what to say, but I don't. I feel like such a failure right now and I know I deserve to."

"Yes you do." And that was all Tasha said before she started to walk out of the office. Harrison caught up with her and gently touched her arm. "You came here to give me another chance today, didn't you?" he asked her. Tasha didn't have to answer him because the intercom on his phone buzzed loudly and Jenna reminded her boss that he is due in court in twenty minutes.

"I have to go, so I'll see you at home?" Harrison asked her and she nodded her head yes. While Harrison was inside of his office collecting the contents for his briefcase as he prepared to leave for the courthouse, Tasha walked by Jenna's desk again. And that's when Jenna stopped her and lowered her voice.

"Mrs. Wheelan, I don't know if you are going to know what I'm talking about but there was a man in here a few minutes ago. He told me he saw your car outside asked to give you a message. Meet Jack Williams at Wally's Diner on Main Street as soon as you can. Tasha's eyes widened. "He was here?" she asked her husband's secretary and she nodded her head. It is none of her business if the *hot guy* who stepped off of the elevator ten minutes ago is someone Mrs. Wheelan is seeing on the side. Jenna knew Harrison had not been faithful to his wife, so she felt like cheering Tasha on with a *you go girl* as she thanked her for the message and exited the office.

Tasha drove directly to Wally's. She had only been there once before when her children talked her into going there for lunch. It is noted for being a fabulous burger restaurant, but Tasha couldn't have cared less about eating anything right now. She also should not have cared about seeing Jack, and hearing him try to explain why he had kept from her the fact that he has a wife and two beautiful little girls who are growing up without him. She knew she should ignore his message, but because he had made such an effort to track her down, she would at least hear what he has to stay.

When she walked into the busy restaurant, she immediately spotted him sitting alone at a table in the middle of the room. He stood up and as she walked over to him she noticed his long bangs, his jeans and cowboy boots and charcoal gray short-sleeved t-shirt. "Please sit down," he offered, and she did.

"You sure went through a lot of trouble to find me today, especially considering you have house guests to entertain."

"I couldn't let you walk away hurt and angry, possibly never seeing you again, not without explaining things," he said as a waitress brought them two plates of burgers and fries. Tasha looked at him, surprised, and when the waitress left she spoke. "You were that sure I would come, huh? Or do you normally eat enough for two?" He smiled at her. He loved her sense of humor.

"I hoped you would come, and I'm thankful you

Timing

did. Tasha, I know today was a shock. Brooklyn never told me they were coming to Baltimore. They flew from Texas, rented a mini-van and showed up unannounced right when you and I could have been–"

"You're telling me! My God, Jack, I had no idea. I thought you were unattached, you only mentioned being in a complicated relationship back in Texas. I hardly call a wife and children a complicated relationship."

"Brooklyn and I are estranged."

"And so you choose to live thousands of miles away from your girls?"

"It's not like that," Jack answered. "They are better off without me in their lives."

"I don't believe that," Tasha said to him. "From what little I do know about you, I know you are a good man. And after seeing them run to you this morning, they obviously love you. How can you be apart from them?"

"It's a long story," he replied.

"Why do you do that to me? You're obviously choosing to keep things from me when you close off like that, but you wanted me here to talk, so fucking talk to me!" Tasha purposely had kept her voice down, but the crowd in the restaurant was loud so she didn't hold back expressing herself with foul language because she felt angry. She pushed her plate forward. She was in no mood to eat.

"I have fallen in love with you. How's that for communication?" Jack's words took her by surprise.

"You are too young for me, we're both married, we both have children, and you are the one who told me if we were to get together, it would just be sex," Tasha was feeling frazzled now. She had just left her husband who begged her to reconcile, but he could have a child on the way with another woman. And now she is with Jack, a man she has come to care about and depend on. But, he's married with children and who knows what other secrets he's keeping from her.

"I do not love Brooklyn. She's only my wife on paper."

"And your children?"

"They are not my children." Jack said, looking down at the plate of food he too had not attempted to eat.

"What? Are you lying to me? I was there, they called you *daddy*, you responded." Tasha felt annoyed and confused and she just wanted to get up and walk away from this man. For good.

"My brother died three years ago when Ava was a

Timing

baby. He made me promise to always take care of his girls, including Brooklyn. I was devastated to lose Neil, so I stepped into his life, with his family. Brooklyn convinced me to marry her, right away, for the girls' sake. I thought it was the right thing to do at the time, but I don't love her. I never have. She knows she is set for life financially, but I just can't be a part of that family anymore. I'm not happy there."

"So that's why you've been back and forth living there and here, and also why you jumped at the chance be with your father this summer?" Tasha asked him, attempting to put all of the pieces together.

"That's part of the reason, yes, I mean I wanted to be with him, but now I just don't know where I belong." She had no idea Jack was dealing with such turmoil in his life. He had seemed, to her, like he couldn't be more carefree. He, in fact, had been the one to remind her of what it feels like to relax and just let go.

"Yes I know the feeling," Tasha said as she now realized why the two of them have been so drawn to each other. They are in the same boat. Two peas in a pod. They understand each other because they are both struggling to make puzzle pieces fit in their lives that just won't slip into place so easily anymore. No matter which way they turn it, or how hard they force it.

"Brooklyn and the girls are only going to be here for a few days," he told her, "so will you come back out to the grounds again after that?" That was a lot for Jack to ask of her, he knew, and Tasha had an answer for him.

"I was at my husband's office today because I decided our marriage is worth fighting for, no matter who or what gets in the way. I'm hoping with every fiber of my being that the baby is not his, but right now I really feel like I need to try harder and even respond to Harrison's pleas for me to meet him halfway in order for us to survive this," Tasha explained.

"You ran to him because I hurt you," Jack said, feeling like this is the end of the road for them. Their friendship. Their budding relationship that he really wanted to make happen. He could see in her eyes how determined she is to make her marriage work. "Brooklyn showed up and you witnessed a family I abandoned coming back for me. You saw no room for yourself in my life and you bolted, back to him. It's wrong to go back if that really isn't where your heart is." Tasha could hear desperation in his voice and it pained her, but she was going to do what she had to do right now. For him. She couldn't allow him to love her. She is not free to love, and neither is he.

Timing

"I'm going to give everything I've got to make my marriage work, and I'm going to walk away right now with an abundance of strength that you have given me, Jack Williams. We were meant to cross paths, for sure, but we are not meant to be." As she said those final words to him, she stood up and he grabbed her hand and stood up too. The wooden chair legs on his chair squeaked loudly on the floor, catching the attention of a few people around them in the restaurant. But he never noticed. And neither did she. Because when they are together, they always feel as if they are the only two people in the world.

And that's what made it extremely difficult for Tasha to pull her hand away from his intense grip and walk away, leaving him standing alone at the table in the middle of that restaurant.

CHAPTER 15

Exactly seven days have passed since Tasha saw Jack. She had gone a week without seeing him before, but this time the distance was torturing her. She missed him. She didn't want him to think she had judged him for leaving his brother's family behind in Texas. But, really, she did not understand how he could walk away from those two little girls who call him *daddy*. The more Tasha thought about Jack's situation, the clearer Harrison's dilemma became. He too wanted to turn his back on a child, a child that could be his, but he hoped is not. Sarah Loft had kept her distance from Harrison since Tasha showed up in his office that day. Both Harrison and Tasha knew she would be back. It was only a matter of time.

Timing

Harrison was packing his suitcase for a weekend business convention in New York City. Tasha didn't want him to leave, because she found herself doubting him and he read her mind when he saw her face as she walked into their bedroom. His suitcase was lying open on the end of their bed and he was putting the last of his things in it when Tasha walked over to him and sat down next to his suitcase. "Are you sure you have to go to New York this weekend? I'm thinking I want you to take me with you. Who cares if Spence has a baseball tournament all weekend? I want all three of us to go so we can meet up with Ari and spend some time together as a family."

"We will do that very soon, Tash, but this trip is going to be hectic and I don't know if I will even have time to see Ari. And you know Spence is not going to skip a baseball tournament just to see his sister." Harrison smiled at his wife.

"Call me when you have a free minute here and there, okay?" she said, feeling needy and she knew she appeared vulnerable to him.

"I will," he said. "You know I miss you already." Tasha felt tears fill her eyes as she allowed Harrison to pull her close. He wrapped his arms around her, pressing his body close to hers. They had talked at length in the last week about trying to make their marriage work, and beginning to deal with Sarah Loft and her baby on the way. Tasha had yet to come back to their bed. She told him she isn't ready, and he reassured her it is okay, he will wait however long she needs. And that is what worried Tasha. Would he really wait? Is he truly through being with other women? She didn't trust him and this trip stressed her out.

***

Tasha was sitting at Spence's game, enjoying the time spent chatting with the other mothers and watching her son pitch flawlessly. He had improved this summer after receiving bi-weekly private pitching lessons. Spence is small for his age, but he can pitch fast and as the coaches have said, time and again, he can pitch strikes. Tasha and Harrison felt extreme pride watching their son. It warmed her heart to see Harrison thrive at fatherhood, it always has. But now it also pained her when she thought of the baby on the way which could possibly be her husband's. She didn't want him to father anyone else's children but hers.

When the game ended, Spence and his friend Cade Carter walked up to her at the same time. Cade's mom Stacy was seated next to Tasha. The boys asked their mothers in unison if Spence could spend the night at the Carter's house. Tasha reluctantly agreed. She was looking forward to some bonding time with her son while

Timing

Harrison is out of town, but her plans for pizza and a movie at home would have to wait. She did insist for Spence to return home with her after the game to take a shower, put on some clean clothes and pack his toothbrush. Within thirty minutes, Tasha had already been home with Spence and dropped him off at the Carters. As she was driving out of their subdivision, she remembered she is out of wine at home and decided to stop at the liquor store on Main Street to pick up a bottle. She rarely drank alcohol in front of Spence, so tonight a couple of glasses of red wine sounded nice. Tasha needed to relax. She had heard from Harrison a few times since he left yesterday morning. His trip is busy but the time is going fast for him, he told her, and then reminded her how much he misses her.

When Tasha left the liquor store, it was already dark outside. She held the bottle of wine as she walked to her car. Downtown is always busy and well lit so she never gave a second thought to it not being safe for her to be out alone in this area at night. Not until she got to her car and saw a man leaning up against her driver's side door. Before she had a chance to be frightened, she recognized Jack. "Awful late for a pretty girl like you to be out alone, don't you think?" He wasn't slurring his words, but Tasha could tell he has been drinking. And then she noticed his truck parked a few spots away from her car, near a popular bar on Main Street. "How much have you had to drink, Jackson Lance Williams the third?" She asked him and he smiled at her for remembering his full name. "Not enough to feel better about losing my best friend."

"Stop. Let's get you out of here, come on, hop in. I'm taking you home. You can get your truck tomorrow because there is no way I'm letting you drive tonight." Tasha pulled him by the arm and away from leaning up against her car door as he walked around to the passenger side. She drove him home, sharing small talk about Harrison being out of town, Spence's baseball tournament and sleepover. When they reached the house on the hill behind the cemetery, Tasha shifted her car into park and kept it running. She was waiting for him to get out of the car, but he didn't.

"You aren't going to see to it that I make it safely inside...tuck me into bed maybe? His eyes were twinkling and Tasha was melting inside. *What a beautiful man. Sexy as hell...and oh dear Lord I need to drive out of here. Now.*

"I think you can handle that, big boy," Tasha said patting him on the leg and he touched her hand, taking it into his. "Come in for a cup of coffee with me."

"I just bought a bottle of wine," she said, "and I really should go home."

Timing

"To an empty house? Mine is empty too, again. The girls were broken-hearted when they left. Brooklyn never learns. She needs to keep them away from me so it's easier to forget."

"I disagree," Tasha said, "It's not that easy to forget you."

"I will make you a promise, pretty girl," Jack said. "Come inside for a little while and be my friend. No intimacy, just talking. I've missed your face."

"Deal." Tasha turned off her car and got out of it with him and they walked inside together to share coffee between friends.

***

It was eleven-thirty when Tasha was driving back home. She and Jack had talked for two and a half hours. She always lost all track of time with him. He told her how difficult it had been for him to spend time with the girls again and then let them go. Tasha reminded him how he didn't have to let them go, he could be in their lives, but he said a life with Brooklyn is not what he wants for himself. And Brooklyn had made it very clear to Jack during her visit that he is the one who left them and he is to never come back unless he wants a life with all of them. It was an ultimatum and Jack didn't want any part of her game. He knew she wanted him for herself more than she wanted him to be a father to her girls. Why couldn't he just be their uncle? That confirmed for Jack exactly what he has always thought about her character. She is a *selfish bitch* and he intended to finally file divorce papers. He definitely felt like he let his brother down by not keeping his promise to take care of his family, but he just could not do it. Jack told her how his brother died and it pained Tasha to imagine it. The two brothers had been together on the eleven acres of land in Texas where Neil lived with his young family. Brooklyn was inside of the house with their girls, while Jack and Neil decided to be boys and play around on their ATVs. There was one helmet for the two four-wheelers. The second helmet had been in the shed or misplaced. Jack had a helmet on his head as they started their engines. Before they moved, Jack raised his voice over the noise and told his brother to go back for his helmet. *My head is harder than yours, big brother* were the last words Jack had heard him say before they took off. Neil rarely wore a helmet, and Jack knew that, so he had not pressed him further. They rode fast on the open land and then dangerously wild through the trees, weaving in and out. Jack never knew how it happened, but he heard the crash and when he looked behind him, he saw his brother had driven directly into a tree. The force had thrown him through the air and when Jack rushed to him, he instantly knew it was not good. There was a growing pool of blood underneath his brother's head. Jack took one

Timing

of his hands and brought it around to the back of his head, and his once hard head was soft. Like mush. It was absolutely the most terrifying feeling Jack had ever experienced. He didn't need to be a doctor to know his brother's head injury was going to take his life. He knew there was no time to call 911 or rush back to the house to get Brooklyn. He wanted to be there when his brother left this world. He didn't want him to be alone. So he cradled him. He cried. He begged him not to go. And his younger brother's last words before he closed his eyes and slipped away were *please take care of my family for me.*

After hearing the heart-breaking story from Jack, Tasha now understood and agreed he needs a life of his own, a place where he truly wants to be. He should not feel obligated to stay with Brooklyn and his nieces out of guilt, or duty to his brother. She wondered if Jack would one day return to Texas to settle down or if he truly wanted stay in Baltimore, or just hide there for awhile. He had not mentioned anything to Tasha and she didn't feel she had a right to ask. Or maybe, she didn't want to know.

Their conversation was powerful tonight and Tasha was still thinking about all of it as she checked her cell phone while driving to be sure she had not missed any calls or texts from Spence or Harrison. She kept her phone with her all night, just in case. It surprised her that she had not heard from Harrison because earlier today when he called, he told her he would call again to wish her a good night's sleep. Trusting him completely again was going to take a very long time.

As she turned into her driveway, she noticed light through the window blinds in the living room. Her heart beat quickened. She wondered if Spence came home from his sleepover early, but he never stayed home alone so why would the Carters not let her know? Then, as the garage door opened up on her side of the garage, she pulled in next to Harrison's car. He was back early from his trip. He never told her he was taking an early flight. He had parked his car at the airport and must have driven home tonight, while she was with Jack.

Tasha was slow to make her way into the house. How full circle this has come, she thought as she is trying, really trying, to trust her husband again and now she is becoming the one in their relationship who cannot be trusted. Nothing happened between her and Jack tonight, but maybe that is beside the point. *She should not be spending time with him on the sly*, she thought to herself as she opened the door in the garage that led up two steps into the kitchen. Explaining to her husband where she has been is going to be a challenge.

She kicked off her shoes, walked through the kitchen setting her wine bottle on the granite countertop, and then she entered the living room and saw him sitting

Timing

on the couch watching a major league baseball game on TV. He was wearing a pair of gray sweat shorts that had become too ratty even for the gym and a navy blue New York Mets t-shirt. His hair was wet and uncombed as if he had just gotten out of the shower. Tasha already knew he had been home for awhile, and probably waiting for her and Spence.

"Well hello," she said, "I saw light in the house when I pulled up and it startled me. Spence is at the Carters for the night and I was not expecting you until tomorrow." He looked at her with an expression she depicted as completely pissed off.

"I had a chance to sneak away from the convention a day early. John stayed. I wanted to get home to my wife. I wanted to show her how much I care about getting our marriage back on track. So I hurried home and found an empty house. Now where in the hell has my wife been on a Saturday night until almost midnight?"

Tasha remained standing in front of the coffee table which was in front of the sectional Harrison was sitting on. He had his bare feet up on that table, crossed at the ankles, and she envisioned him getting so mad at her that he would kick it forward, and toward her. Harrison has never been a violent man, but Tasha was worried she was about to provoke him. "I was at Spence's game, then he was invited for a sleepover with Cade. After I dropped him off at their house, I made a special trip to the liquor store on Main for a bottle of wine. I was in the mood for a glass or two before bed," Tasha felt nervous in the middle of her explanation, "and then I spotted a friend leaving the bar on Main and he was borderline drunk so I drove him home."

"He? So you're telling me you're still seeing the guy in the photographs?" Harrison had called off the private investigator so he had no idea Tasha had been with him again. He just chose to believe she hasn't.

"I'm not *seeing* him, we're friends," Tasha started to explain. "He has been going through a difficult time since his father died and he is estranged from his family so he has no one to talk to." Harrison pulled his feet off of the table and sat forward.

"Tash... I know I have very little room to talk about this, but I rushed home to be with you tonight and when you were not here I knew there was a very good chance you were with him. I have felt fucking ridiculous tonight. My mind kept going there. I don't want to feel like this ever again!" Harrison was yelling and Tasha was not about to hold back. The two of them have been walking on egg shells with each other for the past several weeks, afraid to say too much or even too little because sharing silence had become awkward for them too. They were both afraid of the other giving up. Finally, they were on

Timing

the same page. It was time to let it all out, and Tasha followed suit when Harrison exploded about *his* feelings.

"So let me get this straight... *you* felt ridiculous?" She raised her voice. "Do *you* have any fucking idea how many times I have imagined where you were, who you were with?"

"Is this payback, Tasha?" he interrupted.

"No, it's not. I just wanted to clarify for you how I have felt time and again. Maybe I should tell you about the morning I sat in the parking lot of The Sierra, parked behind your car! I don't have to ask how the food was all night long now do I? Maybe that is where your baby was conceived," she screamed at him, so hard, making her throat instantly hurt.

"Stop it. Don't. We can't do this to each other, Tasha. Come one, we've come so far." Harrison stood up and tried to walk toward her.

"Why do you get all soft on me when I bring up your indiscretions? It hurts doesn't it, Harry? It hurts to picture the spouse you love in the arms of another. Fuck you for thinking I was cheating on you tonight. I was being a friend to someone who has truly been there for me when I needed someone to just listen." Tasha was about to walk away, head upstairs, just get away from him. And he stopped her with his words first, and then his hands on her arms as he turned her around to face him. "Please wait..."

"I need some air," she said to him, "let me go." He released his hands from holding onto her and she left the room and walked outside onto the patio. She was barefoot and she could feel it starting to rain. The patio was under cover but the wind was blowing the rain underneath it. Tasha sat down anyway and when she did she heard Harrison walk out of the house behind her. She didn't turn around, she wouldn't look at him. Not until she heard a clang on the glass table next to her and she turned to find Harrison having dropped his gold wedding band on the table. Her eyes widened as she looked at the ring and then up at her husband. His facial expression was pained. "Take your ring off, Tash."

She looked at her left hand in the dim light that was coming from under the patio and saw her six-carat diamond ring Harrison had given her after he became wealthy enough to afford a diamond of that size. No matter what year it was into their marriage when he gave her that ring, it still represented their twenty years together. She couldn't take it off. She wouldn't. She isn't ready yet. And it suddenly pained her that he is. She stood up quickly, the two of them were both on their bare feet on the concrete that continued to get wet. "No! What are doing?" she felt so panicked.

Timing

"I'm doing what we should have done a long time ago," Harrison answered her. Take off your ring and put it on the table with mine." Tasha just stood there. She was frozen. This is it. This is goodbye to a man she thought she would be married to for life. She turned the ring on her finger, but this was one of those times when she could not move it over her knuckle. She may have been retaining water from not watching her calorie intake as carefully lately and working out a little less faithfully at the gym. She gave it another pull and managed to force it to slide over her knuckle. Her hand was shaking as she set her ring down on the table next to his. She was fighting tears as Harrison used both of his hands to hold her face, and then she released those pent up tears. She rarely cried in front of him anymore.

"So now what?" he asked her, "What do we do? We can walk away or we can begin again." Tasha looked at him, still crying and feeling confused, and he kept talking. "It amazes me, you amaze me how many facets you have. You really do wear your heart on your sleeve sometimes and other times not so much. You're both fragile and fierce. I need to know what you want. I feel like you want to hang in there, you want to bulldoze through the craziness we have in our lives right now. And then tonight happened, and I found myself slapped in the face with the idea that you do care about another man and you are spending time with him. So tell me right now what it is you want. I know I don't deserve a lot from you after all that's happened, but I do need the truth." Harrison picked up both of the rings on the table and handed her his, while he kept hers. "I want us to put these rings back on and start over. Is that what you want too?"

Tasha kept watching him, his face, his eyes, his heart. Yes, she could see his heart. He is the one wearing his heart on his sleeve tonight. And her answer, the one he needed right here and right now, is going to make or break them. She dried her tears with the back of her hand and spoke to him. "Almost overnight, I have watched you become the man you used to be. If you were the same dick you have been to me for so long, I would walk away right now," she actually let out a nervous giggle and he nodded his head as if he agreed. "I know I lost my way too, I know at times I was cold and heartless to you... and I feel like I'm paying dearly for that now with Sarah Loft's pregnancy. If I had paid more attention to loving you and less attention to stepping into that rich bitch persona, I may not have pushed you away." Harrison was listening intently as Tasha continued. "We are both at fault, I'm not going to deny that, and while I did come close to breaking my marriage vows, I did not do it. And I guess the fact that you did do it, burns me, breaks me and does make me want to call it quits with you."

"Let me ask you something," Harrison said so softly

Timing

Tasha almost had not heard him clearly. "Are you going to leave me because I may have gotten another woman pregnant, or is this about him?" Harrison couldn't bring himself to call *him* his wife's new friend as she had called him earlier, because he knew that man has kissed and touched her and he hated him for it. He hated himself too for pushing her into his arms.

"I would be lying if I said the idea of you having a baby is something I think I can handle, but what choice do I have if I want to be with you and remain a family with our children?" Tasha stated. "Just when we thought we were getting another chance, this happens." Tasha sighed, feeling torn. She had only partly answered Harrison's question, ignoring the part about Jack. Did she feel like Jack was holding her back from making a full commitment to her husband? *Maybe.*

"You just said getting another chance, I think it's more about taking a chance," Harrison said to her and she found herself listening so intently to his words. "We will never be one hundred percent sure it will work, but we can be sure that doing nothing, walking away, will not work at all. Most of the time in life you just have to go for it, and no matter how it turns out...just believe it always ends up being the way it should be."

Tasha wondered about the change in him. She was drawn to him, captivated by him, but she found herself feeling skeptical. *What if she jumped in heart first with him again and she ended up getting hurt? Especially if that baby is his. And what about Jack? All logistics aside, he brings something to her life she has never known before. Other than the closeness she shared with her mother, she has never had a best friend. Jack so quickly became that for her. But what if they could share so much more?* Tasha had to force herself to stop thinking about Jack, like that. *He is too young for her. He has ties in Texas. It would be scandalous if she chose him. And who says Jack even wants a life with her? And how would her children fit into that equation? Maybe she owed it to herself to talk to Jack first. Maybe she should take this chance with her husband to start again, because it is the right thing to do. She has children to think about first... and she does love Harrison.*

"I'm here, and I'm always going to be here for you. I love you, Tasha Wheelan." She stopped him, "But, you weren't here for me for so long. There were times I know I reached out and you shut me out."

"That's why we're doing this, we're starting over, making it better," Harrison said, taking her left hand in his and he started to slide her wedding ring back on her finger. "Let me put this ring on your finger as a symbol of the history we share and the best days still to come." Harrison had her heart. He always has. Tasha felt herself sucked in to his world the very first time she laid eyes on him when they met at a mutual friend's party in New York City while they both were college students. She

Timing

again, felt the same pull towards him.

He then reached over onto the table and picked up his ring. Before he handed it to her, he said, "I'm not whole without this ring on my finger or you in my life." That was all it took before Tasha finally caved. She took his ring from him and put it on his finger and at that moment she wanted so badly for him to kiss her and he saw that look in her eyes. He didn't waste another second, he pulled her into passion.

She wanted to feel swept up. She wanted to feel like she hadn't been married for twenty years to a man who had once made her happy and then broke her heart. She knew she did not deserve the wife of the year award, but she also knew she deserved to be loved. She felt herself responding to him, all of him, as they made their way into the house.

They were still kissing and touching and losing their clothes on their way through the living room, with the intention of going up the stairs to their bedroom. They did have the whole house to themselves tonight and that realization came quickly to both of them as Harrison ended on top of her on the floor at the bottom on the stairs. He was making her desire mount as he touched her, kissed her, and gave her repeated attention to pleasure her until she absolutely could not take it anymore. Then he took her as a man takes his wife. She wanted to be his wife, she did. She just didn't know if the hurdles ahead of them would be ones she could make it over without falling down and getting seriously hurt.

CHAPTER 16

The rest of the weekend was bliss for Tasha and Harrison. She, more than he, knew this feeling could be only temporary. This honeymoon-like stage eventually will end. Especially when Sarah Loft continued to hold a key to their happiness.

A few days later when Tasha walked into her husband's office for a planned lunch date, she thought of the last time she had been there. "You're alone this time," she said, making a point to have a conversation about *her*.

"She hasn't been back since, Tash, if that's what you're asking." Harrison stood up from behind his desk, walked to meet her in the middle of the room and he kissed her full on the lips. She giggled, and said, "I guess we could go home for lunch." It had been a very long time since the two of them dined in public together *just because* and Tasha was looking forward to it. Knowing Harrison was dressed in a suit and tie, she pulled her favorite black skirt out of the closet, about two inches above the knee, a sleeveless teal silk blouse with a scoop neckline, and black stilettos. She felt classy today, and she felt loved.

"Will you tell me if she returns and what she has to say," Tasha bore her eyes into his. "I have a right to know, too."

"Of course I will tell you." And that was the full extent of their conversation about Sarah Loft. She is more than a sore subject for them. Tasha saw her as the deal breaker between them, if her baby turns out to be Harrison's.

***

What Harrison didn't tell Tasha is when he returned to work after lunch, he called Sarah Loft and asked her to come to his office as soon as possible. Exactly two hours later, she walked in. She still had not looked pregnant, but she did mention how her clothes are

Timing

beginning to feel tight as she is twelve weeks along. He didn't want to talk about any of that with her, because he didn't want to concern himself with her pregnancy. Sarah Loft remained adamant about not doing any DNA testing until after the baby is born. Harrison had asked her again, and that is when he presented an offer to her which he believed she could not refuse. He told her he will pay her one million dollars. She didn't even have to prove that the baby is his. He didn't want to know either way. He just wanted her out of his life. With that kind of money, he told her she could move anywhere she wanted, have her baby and live a very comfortable life. He wanted absolutely no part of the baby's life. He did not want to know if it's his. All he wanted to do is tell his wife that it is not, and then they could move on with their lives.

    Sarah Loft had been thrown by his offer. She could not believe he never wanted to know, and she warned him about lying to his wife. *If he wanted to make his marriage work, lying is not the answer.* And then the idea of having that much money, and being able to give her baby everything, overcame her. She agreed. She accepted Harrison's offer. She never wanted him anyway. She also did not want the other two men who could have fathered her baby. In fact, she hadn't even told them. One, was a one-night stand after getting drunk in a bar with him, and the other is just a friend with benefits with whom she has occasional sex. Originally, she had hoped Harrison fathered her baby because she cared about him. Now, it no longer mattered to her to have him in her life, she only wanted her baby. A chance to have a baby was something she never thought would be possible for her, and now she was going to be both a mother and a very wealthy woman. Suddenly, Harrison's bank account mattered. Harrison gave her his word. He will write her that check after she has the baby. She is to contact him then, and only then. Not before, and not again after the baby is born. He will pay her one million dollars to leave him out of it. When Sarah Loft closed his office door behind her, Harrison thought never seeing her again, never knowing the truth about her baby, will soon make him a free man. Free to remain married to the only woman he has ever loved.

***

When Tasha left downtown Baltimore, she had flowers on her front seat. She and Harrison had talked about what day it is. Her mother's birthday. She would have been sixty-eight. They reminisced about her, but Tasha never mentioned putting flowers on her grave. She knew Harrison expected her to stay away from the cemetery now and that notion seemed so crazy because her mother is buried there. But Jack also lives so close-by. She would just drive in there, place the flowers and only stay for a few minutes.

Timing

Tasha laughed at herself walking through the grass near her mother's grave in a dress and heels again. She remembered the last time she did, it was the day she met Jack. A part of her really wanted to see him out there today but she noticed the grass had been mowed, probably just the day before, and he was nowhere around.

"*Happy Birthday, mom,*" she said, feeling like she could have cried. "*You know you should be here, you would have enjoyed lunch with us. Things are good, mom. Harrison and I are starting over. He's really trying...and we will have some struggles ahead but I guess we will just deal with that when it happens.*" As Tasha was talking, she heard a sound in the distance and noticed a four-wheeler coming down the rock road from Jack's house. The rider was wearing a helmet and she knew it was him. That body in jeans and a sleeveless t-shirt again was simply enough to send tingles throughout her body. He pulled right up to her, and shut off the engine. She watched him remove his helmet, and then push the long bangs back and out of his face. "New wheels Jackson?" she asked him, surprised he still wanted to ride after the accident, but she tried to sound playful and he seized her up. "No, same one I've always had, I brought it with me from Texas. I never stopped riding, if that is what you're wondering," he paused and then quickly changed the subject. "Pretty girl, why are overdressed like you were the first time I saw you out here?"

Tasha smiled at him, "I know. I just came from a lunch date and I wanted to make sure I brought my mother some flowers today. It's her birthday."

"I see. Happy Birthday, Mary Collins," Jack said looking over at her tombstone. He noticed the sadness in Tasha's eyes and immediately wanted to take it away. "Hop on, you need to clear your mind."

"You can't be serious! Not in a skirt and these heels... and I really should not be spending so much time with you anymore, Jack. I can't." Tasha recommitted herself to her husband and being with Jack felt wrong now. At least her head was telling her no, but her heart was again feeling so open and willing with him.

"You can do it, pretty girl. Come on, I dare you..." Jack had that twinkle in his eyes again and Tasha caved. "On one condition, take me to the house. We have to talk about us."

"Oh so now there's an us?" Jack teased her as she did her best to pull up her short skirt, swinging one leg over the seat, and straddling behind him. He turned around and saw her struggling not to reveal too much leg, or anything else and he giggled as he started up the four-wheeler and gave her his helmet. "Put this on, I insist, or I'm not moving." Tasha did as he asked and he carefully drove them back up to the house. Tasha felt her arms

Timing

tighten around his middle as he picked up speed. She was comfortable. Too comfortable feeling him so close to her.

When they reached the house, Jack got off of the four-wheeler first and then turned around to glance at her before he helped her off. He thought she looked *sexy as hell*. He invited her inside, and she followed. Once they stepped into the house, she slipped off her stilettos and walked over to the couch and sat down. Jack followed her and smiled as she crossed her bare legs. He touched her on the knee and then moved his hand all the way down to her foot. He pulled both of her legs over his lap, turning her toward him on the couch, and he started to massage her feet. "Those fancy high heels must do a number on these cute little feet," he said using all of his fingers and the palms of his hands to rub them. She wanted to stop him, but *damn it felt good*.

"We need to talk, Jack," Tasha didn't want to, but she pulled her legs off of his lap. "Harrison and I have reconciled. We are starting over because we both want to make our marriage work." Tasha was looking at him, and he raised one eyebrow.

"So you're okay with him getting another woman pregnant? What happens when the baby is here?" Jack's words stung, but she expected his directness.

"No, of course I'm not *okay* with it, but I love my

husband and I know how this is killing him. He wants me and our children, we are a family." Tasha sounded as if she was trying to convince herself of that. And Jack didn't buy it.

"When did this happen? Last time we talked, over coffee, you were so unsure." Jack remembered her telling him she was sleeping in her daughter's vacant bed. He wondered if that had also changed as he tried to erase the image from his mind.

"The night I was here, very late. I came home to find Harrison had returned early from his business trip. I was caught off guard, he was angry. We fought, and for the first time in a very long time we laid all of the cards on the table. I was ready to walk away, but I didn't know if I had it in me. I don't know if I'm strong enough sometimes, and I also want to keep my family together. I mean, the baby may not even be Harrison's."

"So you fought and you gave in?" Jack asked, sounding pissy.

"I gave my husband another chance, because we both want to make it right this time."

"Well okay, I'm happy for you." Jack said, sounding anything but.

"Are you? I mean you sound upset or annoyed with

Timing

me?" Tasha pressed him.

"I know some women do that, they keep going back to their scum of the earth men for whatever reasons," Jack said, clearly annoyed.

"Please don't make me feel like *some* woman who is submissive to her husband. I went through that difficult stage and I feel very confident in how I've overcome that. I'm stronger than I realized and I do love my husband."

"Then why are you here with me?" he snapped at her.

"Because...I don't know. Why am I here?" Tasha asked him. "Why do we always make our way back to this point? Real conversation between two people who became instant friends is very hard to walk away from, if you must know how I feel."

"What else is hard to walk away from, Tasha?" Jack moved closer to her on the couch. "I think we both feel it. We've both tried to deny it. You say I'm too young for you. You remind me that you have a family. I don't want to take responsibility for my brother's family in Texas and I carry guilt because of that. And the list goes on. We have found every excuse not to give in, not to go with what has been right in front of us for so damn long."

Tasha felt incredibly frazzled with him now. He

was pushing her, pushing them together, and at this point she doubted she was strong enough to resist him. She had to though. *She had to dammit. She would not do this to Harrison.* "It would just be sex," she said, reminding him of his own words and he smiled at her.

"I think that may have been the case a few months ago, but now I know you, I know your heart. You are not a woman who opens up to a man the way you have with me, not without real feelings going on inside."

"Stop, Jack. This could never work, and I would be no better than my husband who I am working very hard to forgive right now, if I let myself be with you." Tasha stood up from the couch and started to walk away from him. He jumped up and caught up to her halfway across the room. He pulled her by the arm and turned her around to face him.

"You are so beautiful inside and out," he said with softness in his voice that instantly stirred her. "And you've brought something into my life that has been missing for far too long. Fun. I have fun with you, and I don't want to stop. If it means we have to keep this relationship strictly platonic, then so be it. Just don't walk away and never come back. I want to know how you're doing and if you're happy. I want you to throw on some play clothes and take a real four-wheeler ride with me next time so we can feel the wind in our hair together."

Timing

"I'm not so sure we should be feeling anything together anymore," Tasha said wanting to hold on to their newfound friendship so badly, but their intense feelings for each other would eventually surface and get in the way of just having fun.

"You don't trust me?" he asked.

"With my life," she answered. "It's me I don't trust." And then she turned and walked away. She slipped into her stilettos by the door and before she walked out, Jack said, "Come back again, okay?"

She didn't say anything in response, but she knew she would. And so did he.

CHAPTER 17

Tasha and her family were outside in their backyard, including Ari. She finally came home for a visit. The last time she had been home was Christmas and now it was early August. She had seen both of her parents, during their separate visits to New York City, but she had not seen her little brother in person in almost eight full months. She did enjoy skyping with him, sometimes daily, but it had not been the same as pulling him close for a tight squeeze, or squatting down into a catcher's position as he practiced his pitching with her. Ari had played softball since she was old enough to hold a bat, so she could hold her own when Spence pitched his fast balls to her in the backyard and that is exactly what the two of them were doing now as their parents watched them from underneath the patio.

Timing

The feeling of having them all together like this was incredibly fulfilling for Tasha, and Harrison was enjoying seeing happiness on her face. "You're beaming, you know?" he said to her as she grinned at him and felt her eyes get a little teary behind her large dark sunglasses.

"I can't help it, my kids are both here, you're here...I feel so complete." Tasha meant those words from the very bottom of her heart and Harrison leaned in from his chair to hers and kissed her. He told her he loved her as the kids walked up to the patio. Spence immediately recruited his dad to be on the receiving end of more of his pitches as Ari poured herself a glass of iced water from the pitcher on the table and then sat down near her mother.

"You and dad sure seem close. I mean wow, I can feel the love just watching you two and to be honest, I don't remember a time when I felt like you two even liked each other. Dad basically ignored you, and you always seemed to be either trying too hard to get his attention or not at all interested in making any effort." Tasha listened intently to her daughter's words. She felt sad and relieved at the same time. Sad for all of the years wasted, and relieved for the current happy state of their marriage, and their family.

"I'm sorry, honey, I know it used to be downright miserable at times, actually most of the time. I just hope we are making up for all of that now, and I also hope this means you will come home more often. I mean, come on, look at the fun we've had together this weekend," Tasha said throwing her hands and feet up in the air kicking off her flip flops and sending them into the air, finally landing in the grass about fifteen feet in front of them. Ari giggled and replied, "I hope to come home more, mom. But, there is also someone back in New York City who I am enjoying sharing all of my free time with."

Tasha pulled her sunglasses down from her eyes and rested them low on her nose. "Are you telling me you have a boyfriend?"

"Yes, his name is Blake and he also is a business major. We have a lot of our classes together and we clicked from the moment we met. I really like him, mom." Ari's words made Tasha feel both excited and worried. Her daughter dated in high school, but has never been in a serious relationship with a boy.

"Ari, have the two of you...?"

"Yes."

Tasha felt reassured knowing her daughter has been on an oral contraceptive since she was a sophomore in high school. She suffered from an ovarian cyst and the gynecologist had suggested she be on the pill to reduce the size of the cyst and eventually dry it up. It had simply been a water cyst but it was causing Ari continuous

Timing

discomfort. The pill took care of the health issue and Ari continued to take it because Tasha knew eventually the day would come when her daughter would be sexually active. She just didn't know if she would be ready for that day. "I see, okay, um, is this awkward? Because I don't want it to be. I am so happy you feel comfortable sharing this huge event in your life with me. I want you to feel loved and special as you've officially become a woman."

Ari wanted to roll her eyes, but she didn't, because she is so in love with Blake and did feel all of that with him. In addition, she could not possibly feel any more love for her mother than she does at this very moment. Tasha had changed so much in the last few months and Ari wanted that woman to stay. "No, surprisingly, this isn't awkward. It's all so good, mom. I want you to share my joy about this and yes you should know I am in love. This is not just about having sex." Tasha got up out of her chair and bent down to embrace her daughter. When she pulled apart from her, she grew serious.

"Stay on the pill, Ari. Be smart about it. Do not miss a pill, use back-up protection if you are ever on an antibiotic. Just be safe, okay? The last thing you, or Blake, need is a baby!"

"I know all of that, mom," Ari said. "We've talked about that and believe me Blake knows to be responsible because his mom was nineteen when she had him. He has a stepdad now, but Blake's mom raised him alone for the first ten years of his life. She struggled, and he never wants to put himself or a child through that. We both want to be finished with college and established in our careers before we bring a baby into this world."

"Oh my, you two are very serious about sharing a life together," Tasha said, knowing what it feels like to be young and in love. So many times people get caught up in the newness of love and sex and just the idea of planning a future, achieving great career goals, sharing a home and having babies. If only life were that simple, Tasha thought to herself. "I'm extremely happy for you, Ari. You have grown into an amazing young woman. Just please do not make me a granny before my time!" The two of them laughed together as the boys continued to focus on baseball in their yard.

"Speaking of pregnancy, have you heard about the unexpected one in this city?" Ari asked as Tasha waited to hear the name of a former classmate of Ari's or someone else she knew. "The barber downtown. Her name is Sarah Loft. I went to high school with her sister, Kate when we first moved to Baltimore, she was a year older than me but I remember her. Everyone knows Sarah Loft sleeps around and now the rumor is she doesn't even know who the father is." At that moment, Tasha felt as if the baseball being thrown across her backyard had hit her right in the

Timing

stomach. It may as well have, because she had the overwhelming feeling of having the wind knocked out of her.

"I had not heard that," she said, trying to recover. "I only know of her, so her reputation is not something I've concerned myself with. You know how I feel about gossip, Ari."

"Sorry, mom. I just found it kind of funny how she doesn't even know who she slept with and when." Ari giggled, and Tasha swallowed hard. Just like that, their perfect afternoon had turned sour. The mere mention of *her* name and *that* baby on the way had sent Tasha reeling again.

***

When Tasha walked into their bedroom later that night, she was carrying a glass of wine. She could hardly wait to pour herself a glass, or two, tonight. Her conversation with Ari was still very front and center in her mind.

Harrison looked at her from across their bedroom. "What's wrong? I saw you talking to Ari this afternoon, it looked serious, and you've seemed a little far away tonight. Everything okay with her?" He was sitting up in bed, reading over a court case that he wanted to be on top of his game with next week. His chest was bare as he was wearing only his silk pajama bottoms, the maroon colored ones, tonight.

"You can read me that well, huh?" She asked him as she walked over to the end of their bed and took a few sips of her wine before responding. "Well, first, Ari has a boyfriend, Blake whom she also told you about and well they are having sex." Harrison dropped the papers onto his lap in bed and sat up straighter. "What? Oh for chrissakes! I don't want to hear this. Geez, I know she is a young woman, but no dad wants to be aware of that."

"It really is okay, she is being very responsible." Tasha informed him.

"So that's not what is bothering you?"

"No, I'm bothered by the fact that Baltimore is circling with rumors about the whore who cuts hair and bends over for every other man who walks into her shop." Tasha was angry again. Still. It's not like she has ever been able to let go of the fact that her husband screwed up and their family could still fall apart because of it. She has, however, been able to put that fact far into the back of her mind sometimes. She had to, in order to function day to day. Not hearing from her, not seeing her, and believing that Harrison has not had any contact with her has also helped to temporarily ignore the elephant in the room.

Timing

Harrison looked down at the bed with all of the scattered papers in front of him. He, without a doubt, felt like he failed his wife and his family. But he also felt confident in his plan to keep Sarah Loft and her unborn baby out of his life in order to keep his family intact.

"Who is talking about her?" Harrison asked.

"Our daughter asked me if I had heard. Do you have any idea how that made me feel? I know my husband was one of those men who may have fathered the town whore's baby. And, God, if Ari knew, her heart would shatter. She adores you."

"Look Tash, I know. Okay? I know. This is going to work out. We are not going to lose our family. That baby is not mine." He sounded over confident and Tasha immediately questioned him.

"Until the tests are run, you don't know anything for sure." She finished her glass of wine and left the room to go back downstairs to fill up her glass again. It was early August and there were still six more months to get through before Sarah Loft's baby is due.

Downstairs in the kitchen, Tasha thought of Jack. It has been two weeks since she saw him last, and she missed him terribly. He's the friend she has learned to turn to, confide in, seek advice from. She knew what he would say to her now. She knew he would tell her to get out of her marriage, leave her husband for the pain he is causing her. She also knew he would say that in his own favor, because he now wanted her to be with him. Their friendship had grown, and so had their physical attraction to each other.

***

Ari had already left for her three-hour drive back to New York City on Monday morning and Harrison was at work for a few hours already. Tasha was about to walk out the door with Spence, who was participating in a golf camp this week, when her cell phone rang. She picked it up off of the kitchen table, noticing the call from Thomas-Wheelan Law Firm.

She said *hello*, already knowing it is Harrison. "Tash, John and I need you to rescue us today." John Thomas and Harrison met in law school and John is the one who came up with the idea for them to combine their talent and create success together, which prompted Harrison to move them from New York City to Baltimore and join John Thomas in starting up Thomas-Wheelan Law Firm. "What? You and John?" Tasha had no idea what Harrison meant as she motioned for Spence to put on his shoes in the kitchen so they could get moving and get him to golf camp on time.

"Jenna had to leave this morning and she is going

to be out the rest of the week for sure. We have no secretary and no substitutes are available. The phone has been ringing off the hook and well I'm asking you to help us out."

"Harrison, I know nothing about keeping things afloat at your law firm." Tasha was giving Jenna well-deserved credit. Without her, she knew both Harrison and John were simply helpless. They may be brilliant lawyers but neither one of them knew how to keep a schedule or work the copier.

"That doesn't matter right now, all you have to do is pick up the phone, direct a call or take a message. Please?"

"Give me at least a half an hour to take Spence to golf camp and to get myself ready," she said, wishing she had not agreed to *work* for him.

"Thank you! I owe you, honey. See you soon." Harrison hung up the phone and Tasha hurried her son out the door.

***

When she arrived at the law firm, she quickly found a parking spot and got out of her car to walk into the building. She had chosen a long, flowy black skirt and a sleeveless white cashmere sweater. She had added a chunky silver necklace and bangle bracelet to compliment her outfit. She also had worn her favorite red stilettos. Red meant power and she had giggled to herself when she slipped them on in her closet at home. She was nervous as hell about helping to run the show at Harrison's law firm, but she wanted to help for Jenna's sake. She just decided to wing it and look the part while attempting to.

Harrison was sitting at Jenna's desk when Tasha stepped off the elevator. She couldn't help but grin at him. He looked stressed and out of sorts. "Oh thank God, you're here!" he said as he stood up from behind the desk and she walked over there, too.

"Relax, Harry. It's just a phone." she giggled and he pinched her bottom.

"Remember that after it rings off the hook all day long. John will be here for awhile if you have any questions. I'm due in court soon, but I will be back later."

Tasha sat down, looked at the phone which was currently silent. Then she moved the mouse for the desktop computer. Harrison had pulled up the name of his client on the screen and sent a few documents to the printer. Tasha heard the papers coming out of the printer across the room as Harrison walked over to retrieve those and turned back to her before he walked toward the

Timing

elevator. She watched him attempt to tighten his tie while holding the papers in one hand and his briefcase in the other. "You look made for this job," he said smiling at her and she laughed out loud.

"Liar," she teased him and he left the building.

While Tasha was familiarizing herself with the office, she had answered three calls. Two were for Harrison and she had taken messages. Easy enough. The third call was for John and she found the intercom to buzz into his office and ask him if he could take the call on line one. He did, and once she noticed the red light off again on her phone, she saw John coming out of his office.

"Thank you for saving our asses today, lady," he said, smiling that crooked smile of his and strutting over to sit on the end of Jenna's desk. John always acted overconfident, and to some he seemed arrogant. Tasha, however, knew from how Harrison spoke of him and also from the times they had been together for dinner or public functions, that John Thomas is just a big teddy bear. He, at six-foot-two and two hundred and fifty-five pounds was overweight. His hairline had receded to the point where he should just shave his entire head but he didn't seem to care. He smelled as if he had taken a bath in his cologne this morning as Tasha tried not to inhale too much while he sat directly in front of her.

"You're welcome. I'm not sure what I'm doing, but I will do what I can to get you and Harrison through today and a few other days while Jenna is out." Tasha realized she sounded overconfident now, but she knew John wouldn't see through her pretense.

"Great!" His voice was too loud, almost booming in that office space. "Do me a small favor then before I head out for a meeting."

"Sure," she replied, "what do you need, Johnny?"

John laughed at her and she winked at him. His wife Gabi is a judge and she at five-foot-nine with legs up to her neck is a perfect match for John. She, unlike him, is not overweight but she is definitely solid compared to Tasha's tiny five-foot-three frame. Gabi and John's marriage appeared to be perfect, though childless. They traveled often and the mere idea of them wanting to spend that much time alone with each other was admirable, Tasha thought. She hoped once their kids are grown, she and Harrison will be a couple like that. A few months back that prospect would have been completely out of the question. Now that their relationship has been renewed, Tasha could see the two of them enjoying life as a couple again. That is, if Sarah Loft and her baby do not get in the way. She still could not imagine making room in their lives for a baby. A baby that Harrison fathered with another woman. "Pull up Mary Cooper's file, send the last

Timing

three pages of the document to the printer and I will grab them on my way out." John walked back into his office but Tasha could still smell his unpleasant cologne hanging in the air as she again moved the mouse for the desktop to bring up the application she saw on the computer screen earlier. It appeared all she had to do was plug in a name and retrieve a file. She highlighted the existing name on the file and began to type MARY C-O and that is when the automated program search instantly pulled up the list of Mary C's in the system. Tasha's eyes immediately went to Mary Collins. Her mother's name, and it was in fact her mother's file. There was a legal case against the drunk driver who had crashed into her, and killed her. Harrison built the case and he planned to *nail that killer to the wall.* But Tasha stopped him from filing it. She hoped that man had learned from his deadly choice to drink and drive. She prayed for him once, following her mother's death, and then she put him out of her mind. She had never met him, never even seen him and she didn't ever care to. She slowly clicked on her mother's name. *What would be the harm in reading what Harrison had in that document? Nothing is going to change now. The case that never began was history.* When she opened the document, she read how Harrison was seeking justice to be served for the death of his wife's mother. The man, intoxicated behind the wheel and responsible for the death of Mary Collins, was listed as Jackson Lance Williams III.

Lori Bell

Tasha's eyes widened and her heart felt as if it were in her throat. She put her hand over her mouth and tears immediately sprung to her eyes. *Her Jack? No, it can't be! Jack killed her mother? Jack had been drinking and driving drunk and he took her mother's life that day. He is the reason she lost her mother. He is responsible for how she's grieved and missed her mother more with each passing day. Jack knew all along. She confided in him, she stood with him in front of her mother's grave time and again. That is where they met for the very first time. And he continued to keep the truth from her.* Tasha quickly pulled herself together when she saw John coming out of his office. She minimized the file pertaining to her mother and she hurried to punch the keys on the computer keyboard to retrieve the file on Mary Cooper which John requested. "Your file is printing now," she said to John and he walked over to the printer to wait. "Thanks, Tasha. I will see you in a couple hours."

When John left the office, Tasha sunk down into her chair behind the computer. Her hands were shaking, her palms were perspiring. Jack kept this from her. He's no good. He is a man with secrets. First, she found out he has a wife and kids. And now, the shocking fact that he took her mother's life. It was his choice to drink and drive so he inevitably chose to put other people's lives at risk. And her poor mother lost her life because of Jack Williams. Tasha's mind was reeling. She will confront him. She wanted so badly to take off right now and drive

Timing

directly to the cemetery, find him, and grab him by the shoulders and shake him with all of her strength, begging him to tell her there has been some mistake. He did not kill her mother.

***

It wasn't quite quitting time yet, but Tasha told John she had to leave at four-thirty. She arranged two hours earlier for Stacy Carter to pick up Spence from golf camp and keep him at her house until she was able to pick him up. Harrison was still in court, and John told Tasha to go ahead and leave, anyone who called could leave a message.

Tasha didn't leave Harrison a voicemail message on his cell phone and she didn't drive to the Carter's house to pick up Spence. She just got into her car and raced on the roads to the outskirts of the city to the cemetery grounds. She threw her car into park, got out, and stood at her mother's grave. She openly cried, hoping her mother was not ashamed of her from heaven. She had not only befriended, but had gotten so close to the man responsible for taking her mother's life. She let him into her heart. And he continued to lie to her. Tasha felt like such a fool.

She couldn't find the words to speak to her mother, she just kept crying. Nothing was stopping her emotions, all of the hurt and all of the pain, until she heard his truck turn off the main highway and into the grounds. He spotted her right away and pulled up behind her parked car. And when he got out of his truck, he looked ecstatic to see her. "Well hello, it's been awhile pretty girl!" He walked toward her and noticed her face was red and blotchy and wet with tears. His face immediately lost its smile as he reached for her out of pure concern. He tried to wipe away the tears on her cheeks, and she stopped him. She forced his hand down with her own, and she took one step backwards. "Don't. Don't pretend with me anymore!"

"Pretend? I've never pretended with you. In fact, no one has ever made me feel like being more genuine." Jack's words stung because she knew he has not been completely honest with her.

"So you've never stood right here with me and pretended to be surprised that my mother, the woman who is six feet under this ground I'm standing on," Tasha stomped her red stiletto into the ground a few times, "died because of a drunk driver?"

"Tasha..." he knew then that she is aware he was the man, drunk behind the wheel. He didn't know how she found out, and that didn't even matter to him. This is the day, however, he hoped to God would never come.

"Say it, Jack! Say that you killed my mother!" she

Timing

spat the words at him, feeling like she is supposed to hate him for what he did. Her heart was beating so rapidly and her body was shaking as she stood there in the green grass in her red stilettos.

"I never wanted you to know, especially after I saw you standing here that day. I walked over to you and started talking to you, because I wanted to feel forgiven. I wanted to know you didn't blame me. It pained me more than you will ever know to see you grieving, it still does." Jack pushed his bangs back and out of his eyes as Tasha watched him. That gesture used to make her heart melt, but now looking at him, watching him, and listening to him face this awful truth with her had sickened her. "You have to know when you eventually told me that you were the one who refused to press charges, I wanted to tell you. I wanted to thank you for saving my life, for giving me my freedom. I know I deserved to go to prison then but I had a family, my brother's family, to be there for."

"You left them, Jack! They could not have meant that much to you if you were given a second chance to be with them and then you abandoned them!" Tasha was screaming at him. She honestly had thought she had done some good by not pressing charges, by not fighting for justice for her mother. She remembers the arresting officer informing her how the man who caused her mother's car accident otherwise had a clean record.

Lori Bell

"I am not going to explain this to you again, I thought you understood already. I cannot replace my brother. I want my own life," Jack paused before continuing to speak. It was now or never, he had to fight for her. "I know God put me on this earth for a reason and I used to wonder if I was going to drift around my whole life and never find a purpose. Until I met you." Jack took a few steps toward her and she did not move.

"You have got to be kidding me! Do you realize how absurd this is? You and me? Especially now that I know you are the reason my mother is dead!" The tears returned and she couldn't do it anymore. She could not stand there with him. Everything he had meant to her before was gone. He no longer defined good in her eyes. She started to walk away and he stepped in front of her. "Don't leave like this!" he raised his voice and then she saw the tears on his face. He immediately shifted from being the most masculine image of a man in Tasha's eyes to appearing fragile. "I am so incredibly sorry for keeping the truth from you. Please don't hate me, I hate myself enough as it is. I've always hated knowing I brought other people pain by what I did, and even more so now than I ever could have imagined after meeting you, building a friendship with you, and falling in love with you. I can't take it back, but you have to know I wish I could have traded my life for hers that day."

Timing

"Why didn't you tell me?" Tasha asked him, still feeling so connected to him but she was fighting those feelings with anger. "And how many other secrets are you keeping? Don't even tell me. I don't care. I don't want to know because nothing could be any worse than this one." Her voice was suddenly calm and her face showed no emotion, except for the extreme sadness in her eyes. "Tell me about that day, tell me about the events leading up to you crashing your truck into my mother." Tasha knew, from the accident report, that it had been a full-sized pick-up truck which had crashed into her mother's compact PT cruiser.

"Tasha, please," Jack said, looking down at the ground, moving his tan work boots through the tall grass and still feeling incredible guilt and remorse for putting a human being six foot under them.

"Tell me!" she screamed at him.

"I had just packed up everything I owned in Texas and made another move here. I had only been in town for a few days. My heart was heavy from leaving the girls, but I just could not take Brooklyn anymore. The responsibilities my brother left behind are not mine and I couldn't force myself into *his* world anymore. My father and I had a terrible fight about it and I stormed out and drove to the liquor store on Main. I bought a bottle of whiskey and ended up putting it in my truck and walking into the bar. They finally kicked me out of the bar at three a.m. when they closed their doors, so I sat in my truck and drank the whiskey. I've never had so much to drink in my life. I just didn't want to feel anything anymore. I had let so many people down, I broke my promise to my dead brother."

"My mother was in the accident at eight-thirty in the morning," Tasha interrupted, and Jack continued to explain.

"I slept in my truck for a few hours I guess and all the alcohol I consumed had still not worn off. It was a combination of being intoxicated and being tired. I started driving, I remember not feeling in control at all, and I crossed the center line and I hit the oncoming car head on. I either woke up or came to my senses at the very last possible second...and it was too goddamn late. I've relived that moment a million times and wished I could take it back every second of my life since." Tasha knew her mother had just left the gym in the city. The speed limit leading out of the city on that frontage road is posted at fifty-five miles per hour. The police concluded in the investigation that her mother had been putting along at forty-five miles per hour, and the driver of the truck who hit her had reached a speed of seventy-one before the crash.

"This is a nightmare," Tasha said, glaring at him.

Timing

"How could you not tell me what you did? I cared about you, you son of a bitch!"

"I'm sorry, but I think you already know why I couldn't tell you the truth...because I didn't want to see the way you are looking at me right now." Jack paused, and then he reached out for her hands, but she refused while keeping them at her sides and he took them by force into his anyway. She resisted at first, but then gave in when she looked into his eyes. "You're incredibly shocked and so pissed and so hurt because of me right now, but time will pass and you will clearly see that I am not a heartless man. I am a man who has lived through some serious, crazy shit in my life. And what I have taken away from all of those experiences is knowing no matter what happens, we have to accept things and move on, and believe it will get better." Jack was still holding her hands in his, and she listened to him. "After the accident, I left Baltimore and went back to Texas. I tried to make it work, taking my brother's place again. I spent another two years being unhappy. I know now that I was punishing myself for what I did to your mother. I refuse to live like that anymore. Here, in Baltimore, I've been able to find some peace and being on that path has led me to you. I wish I could take back that day, but I can't." Tasha wanted to free her hands away from his to wipe the tears off of her face, but she just let them freefall. "I remember being a kid and wanting to be older and big enough to do the things adults can do. And then I grew up and found myself wishing I could go back in time when things were so much simpler. As a man now, I've learned how we all need time to accept change, time to heal from hurt and loss, and the timing in which God sets everything in motion on this earth is impeccable. He brought us together for a reason. Don't lose sight of that." Jack let go of her hands and walked away. Without looking back at her, he got into his truck and drove up to the house on the hill. He wanted with all of his being for Tasha to follow him. To forgive him. But, he left her standing there knowing she needed *time*.

    Tasha couldn't move. She just stood there. She wanted to talk to her mother, but there was nothing more to say. Mary Collins was meant to live sixty-five years of life and then move on to greater things. Heaven called her that day, and her mother is most definitely in a better place, despite the fact Tasha needed and wanted her there with her. A reckless decision on Jack's part had literally led him directly into her mother's path on that day. It was timed that way. It seemed awful to believe, but it was out of everyone's hands after Jack became intoxicated and began driving. She wanted to tell Jack that, but she couldn't. Not yet. This was all still extremely too raw. She wouldn't allow herself to drive that windy, narrow road up to Jack's house. She was not ready to let go, or to accept

Timing

this. It was beginning to make crazy sense in her head, but not yet in her heart. And she didn't know if it ever would.

When she turned to walk away, her eyes caught the tombstone from across the path. It was the same tombstone that Jack had been trimming around the very first time she met him and he had spoken to her. She never really walked around or looked at any of the other stones while visiting the cemetery, she had not even read any of the other names. She didn't want to. She didn't care. She thought it was unfair that she had to even step foot in the cemetery, because *her* mother had died and was buried there. Today, though, she was staring at another stone, at the saying engraved on it and she walked closer to be able to read it. She didn't know why, but she felt drawn to it. And as she got closer, she read it.

"*In the end, only three things matter: How much you loved, how gently you lived, and how gracefully you let go of the things not meant for you*" It was a quote, credited to Buddha, etched right there on the stone in front of her. And those words struck her. She instantly believed that message was for her today, right at this every moment. She needed to gracefully let go of Jack Williams because he was not meant for her. He never was.

CHAPTER 18

"So you're telling me the man you toyed with and the man responsible for driving drunk and killing your mother is one in the same?" She had to tell him. Even though she was still in shock, she needed to talk about it, she wanted to tell her husband the truth. No more secrets. If their marriage is going to survive, some changes needed to be made. Starting now.

Timing

"You honestly had no idea his name is in your file?" Tasha asked him.

"I closed that file, years ago, when you didn't want to press charges. I have not looked at it since," Harrison explained. "So have you confronted him?"

"After I left your office today, I drove to the cemetery. I was emotional at my mother's graveside when he drove into the premises. I was so angry, and he was remorseful." Tasha could hardly allow herself to imagine his face, his eyes, and his slumped shoulders as he turned and walked away from her.

"I hope you're done with this *friendship*," Harrison wanted to call it so much more but he didn't. "He is the reason we lost a very special woman, he is the reason our kids are growing up without a grandmother." Harrison was purposely stressing the obvious. He was sad for her pain, but relieved his wife now had a damn good reason to get that man out of her life. For good.

"Stop, okay? I know, and it hurts so much to put a face on the man who took her away from us." It wasn't just a face. Jack is a man whom Tasha had quickly developed genuine, amazing feelings for. She knew his heart, and that made this lie all the more painful. She knew he kept the secret to protect her from more pain and to protect himself from her wrath, as well as the end of their relationship. "I think that was part of the reason why I never wanted to pursue pressing charges. It was better not knowing. I didn't want to see him, or know him. I never wanted to carry that kind of hate for someone, anyone, in my heart." But that wasn't an issue now. Tasha didn't hate Jack, she hated what he did. And she didn't know if she had it inside of her to forgive him. Not for this.

Harrison pulled her close and she lost it in his arms while standing in their kitchen. The dinner dishes were still on the table, on the counter and stove top, and the dishwasher door was hanging wide open. She cried hard for her mother, and she cried even more intensely for Jack. Because she knew, this was it. This was goodbye. Forever.

***

Tasha was lying in bed, listening to it raining outside. A month passed since the day in the cemetery when she confronted Jack. She had not returned to visit her mother's grave or to see him on the grounds, and life resumed as normal at the Wheelan house. She and Harrison continued to put the extra effort into rebuilding their marriage and to keeping it strong. Spence was back in school after a productive summer of sports camps. Tasha had just returned from dropping him off at school. The rain made her feel sad and depressed, so she opted not to go to the gym or take care of any errands. She just

Timing

wanted to go home and crawl back into bed. And that is exactly what she did when she slipped out of her clothes and into the bed. She was wearing only her matching black bra and panties as she pulled the covers over her. The sheets felt cool on her bare skin as she put her head back on the pillow and stared up at the ceiling. The weather turned stormy outside as the rain was downpouring, lightening lit up the room and a thunder crack followed. She had the window blinds wide open in her upstairs bedroom, but the dark skies made it seem more like nighttime than day.

As Tasha lay there in bed, she wondered when these thoughts and feelings were ever going to subside. She didn't like feeling this way. Jack crossed her mind every day, multiple times a day. She was trying to move on, it was just difficult to forget. They had become fast friends and a connection like theirs just doesn't come along often. It still seemed surreal to Tasha to know Jack Williams had been the man behind her mother's untimely death.

She thought again about what he had said to her. About timing. *We all need time to accept change, time to heal from hurt and loss, and the timing in which God sets everything in motion on this earth is impeccable.* Was it really so impeccable how they met, Tasha wondered. And then she answered her own question. *Yes it was.* Jack came into her life when she needed someone most. He indirectly brought her husband back to her. Harrison wised up and realized he could lose his wife so he changed his ways and fought for her. Tasha's relationship with Jack brought both of them a sense of peace, but each in a different way. Jack had admitted to her that he was running away from a life in Texas, where he knew he didn't belong and finding her had given him a purpose. He had fallen in love with her, he told her twice. And she would never forget it. She had wanted to say those words back to him, but refrained. She could not allow herself to take her relationship with him to the next level, not when she still wanted her husband and their family together. She hopes she will always want to fight for her marriage. And she also hoped it will soon become easier to accept how Jack cannot be in her life. Not in any way.

Her cell phone ring tone disrupted her concentration and Tasha noticed Harrison calling. "Hey, have I caught you during your work out?" Tasha had immersed herself back into her daily routine of visiting the gym every morning. It was a way to clear her mind and continue to stay in shape. The few pounds and inches she added to her small frame at the start of summer were now nowhere to be found as Tasha was completely toned again. She simply felt better in her clothes and when she looked into the mirror. And lying there in bed in only her underwear, she looked amazing at forty-five. The sales

Timing

clerk had said as much to her last week when she bought a few pairs of size two jeans at the mall and had to show her identification as part of a random check that particular day when she paid with a credit card. The young female clerk did the math and based on pure admiration had boldly complimented Tasha on her appearance, and of course Tasha was flattered. "No, I'm at home, in bed," Tasha told him.

"Now? What's wrong? Are you feeling sick?" Harrison immediately sounded worried about her.

"No, just lazy I guess." Harrison knew it was not like Tasha to ever return to bed mid-morning, but he did know she has been struggling with the truth about Jack Williams. It was almost as if she was grieving for her mother all over again. He just hoped she would snap out of her slump soon.

"I'm a little envious of your chance to enjoy a lazy rainy day and I wish I could be there with you," Harrison said, smiling into the phone. "I just wanted to call and tell you not to plan on me for dinner tonight. I have a client cocktails and dinner meeting to attend." It's been months since she received a call like this one from Harrison. Those late nights at the office always used to make Tasha doubt him, and for good reason. And suddenly she found herself back there again. Her silence forced Harrison to speak. "Tash, I know what you're thinking and please don't go there in your mind. I've avoided evening meetings for months because I didn't want you to feel the way you're feeling right now. I will be home by eight or nine, okay?"

Tasha swallowed hard on her end of the phone. "Okay. Thank you, Harry." He had no idea how much she needed that reassurance from him. Or maybe he did.

"Focus on the good, Tash. It's going to stay that way, I promise." Harrison's words were still ringing in her ears when they ended their phone conversation. How could everything possibly stay good when Sarah Loft is now in the second trimester of her pregnancy? Tasha flashed to the image of her that she had taken away from their unexpected encounter last week on Main. Tasha had gone to a sub shop to pick up sandwiches to bring to Harrison's office for lunch. She wanted to surprise him with a makeshift picnic lunch on his desktop, but it turned out she was the one who ended up being on the receiving end of a surprise. The two women spotted each other at the same time. Sarah Loft had briefly wondered if Harrison's wife would even recognize her. She had gained twenty pounds and was already showing at almost five months along. Tasha saw her immediately. Every pregnant woman has unfortunately caught her eye in the last few months. She didn't need a reminder of there being a baby on the way who could ruin their lives, but she had one that day when Sarah Loft stopped walking and stood

Timing

directly in front of her on the sidewalk. The foot traffic around them continued to move by as the two women both felt as if the world had stopped and wished for the awkward moment to be over. "Hi," Sarah had said hoping to somehow break the tension. "Hi," Tasha responded, staring at her growing belly, at what could be her husband's baby growing inside of another woman's womb. Tasha was not going to ask her how her pregnancy is going, or how she is feeling. None of that mattered to her. All she could think of is *this woman has been with my husband.* She could have made small talk just to be polite, but her manners were the last thing on her mind as she just started walking past Sarah Loft. She would never wish ill on anyone, especially not an unborn baby, but Tasha felt hateful at that moment. She didn't want to feel it, but a part of her had hoped Sarah Loft would not be able to carry that baby to term. She, again, should have felt ashamed of herself but she didn't. So she kept walking, picking up her pace until she reached the next block and was able to turn a corner and be out of sight from that pregnant woman whose baby could so very easily ruin her life as she knows it.

Later that same day, she was angry at Harrison again and she told him so. He is the reason for all of this, the reason their family could so easily shift from whole to broken when Sarah Loft's baby is born. There had been no more contact between Harrison and her since the day he asked her to come to his office and presented her with the offer she did not refuse. As far as Harrison knew, Sarah Loft remained pregnant and he is prepared to pay her off to say the baby is not his. He did not intend to have any DNA testing done. He just wanted to write her a check and sever all ties. Tasha noticed he seemed unaffected by the news that she had seen an obviously pregnant Sarah Loft, and by the idea of the baby's arrival getting closer week after week, month after month. That day, Tasha finally drilled him about it. "Have you prepared yourself for the fact that the months are passing by quickly and before we know it, it will be any day before she has that baby?"

"I'm prepared to find out that her baby is not mine so we can continue to move on with the rest of our lives together, Tash." Again, his confidence surprised her.

"And what if, for you, the unexpected happens and you do have a baby to love and to raise?" Tasha suddenly wanted to have a plan. Their time of living in denial was only temporary, and no matter how hard she tried to, she could not imagine herself accepting a baby into their lives. Not a baby Harrison fathered with another woman. *Would she leave him? Ask him for a divorce and never look back?* She didn't like how it felt to sever a relationship. All of her life she has been loyal and nurturing, taking great pride in sustaining long relationships. But, she hoped she could be

Timing

capable of surviving on her own. She and Harrison shared more than twenty years together and walking away from that was something she could not fathom. But Tasha, always being the dreamer, had to face reality now. She felt panicked about the baby arriving, the reveal of the test results, and the state of her marriage being in *her* hands. *Was she strong enough to walk away if it comes to that? Or would she have to delve deep for more strength from within to hang on, fight, try harder?*

"I choose you, Tash. We have *our* children and our life together. I don't need anything or anyone else." That should have touched her, but Tasha was overcome with sadness. She never would have ever believed Harrison is a man who would turn his back on his blood.

***

Tasha was dwelling on things she cannot change. She was feeling annoyed with herself for being back in bed, mid-morning. She began to mentally remind herself how she has her health, she has her family. *Focus on the good things, Tasha,* she said aloud to herself as she threw the covers back and got out of bed. She was going to make her bed again and get on with her day, raining or not she had things she should be doing. And that is when her cell phone rang again. This time, it was Ari calling.

"Hi sweets, how is my girl today?" Tasha sounded chipper, but barely had the chance to get those words out before she heard Ari bawling on the other end of the phone. After hearing her say *mom*, Tasha had not been able to understand a single other word in the midst of her daughter's hysterics.

"Ari! Please calm down, take a deep breath, and tell me what is going on." Tasha began to feel panicked, but forced herself to remain calm in order to reach Ari.

"Blake left me. We're done." As Ari said those words, she began to cry again and Tasha's heart broke for her daughter. Her first heartbreak. And Tasha knew her nineteen-year-old daughter is feeling like it is the end of the world.

"Oh gosh, honey. What happened? Your first fight?" Tasha wondered if maybe that is all it was, a fight or maybe an overreaction, and everything would be fine once the two of them had a little space and time to think.

"Hardly," Ari answered.

"So you're saying you two fight a lot?" Tasha carefully asked her, thinking how sometimes getting Ari to open up and communicate is such a challenge.

Timing

"Ever since his mom made him get a full-time job, yes," Ari replied.

"How can Blake be in school full-time and work full-time?" Tasha asked.

"Exactly. That is what I've been telling him for over a month now. He has been going to school all day, every day, and working nights at the grocery store where his mom works. He can't function anymore, he never sleeps and he's extremely edgy all of the time. Not to mention his grades are suffering."

"And his mother wants him to do this?" Tasha asked. "I thought he was going to school on a student loan and living in the dorm? I realize he needs money to live, but why the urgency for him to work full-time now?"

"His mother is fucking crazy," Ari blurted out and Tasha's eyes widened on the other end of the phone.

"Is she really?" Tasha asked.

"No, but she's raised him in such an old-fashioned way. Only buy what you need, never what you want and work your ass off for a measly paycheck." Tasha knew exactly where this was going now and she felt partly responsible. She recognized how her daughter and Blake are from two very different worlds. He came from practically nothing, knowing all too well what it feels like to want for things he will never be able to afford to have. Ari, on the other hand, was born never wanting for anything. Not having enough money was never an issue. Tasha and Harrison had both grown up in middle-class homes so they both understood how to work for things they needed or wanted. Their children, however, grew up beyond spoiled. Neither one of them had done an exceptional job at teaching Ari and Spence the value of a dollar. And now that very truth just might have ruined her daughter's relationship with her first love. Or maybe Blake and Ari just were not meant to be. Tasha needed to speak to her daughter at length, she needed to be there for her and not just through a phone call.

"Ari, I am going to take a little road trip to come see you."

"Mom, you don't have to come. I just needed to hear your voice." Tasha eyes were suddenly teary. She relished this newfound closeness with her daughter.

"I want to. I know you have classes, but we will find the time to talk and maybe I can offer you a little insight or advice to get you through this difficult time."

"Thanks, mom." Ari was crying again, but promised her mother she would be fine as they talked just a few minutes longer before Tasha ended their call to start packing for a quick trip to New York City.

Timing

While she was throwing her clothes into an overnight bag, Tasha called Harrison at his office. She explained to him how he needed to take care of Spence for a day or two and she was planning to ask the Carters to help before and after school. At first, Harrison seemed annoyed by Tasha's rash decision to rush to New York City, but then Tasha emphasized how much it means to her to be building a stronger and closer relationship with their daughter. He said he understood, wished her safe travels on the road, and then told her he loves her.

This is what life is about, Tasha thought as she finished packing. She believed with all of her heart in being there for her children. And now that she is finally feeling the love and support of her husband, she just knew everything else will work itself out.

CHAPTER 19

Being in New York City most definitely felt like going back home for Tasha. After three hours on the road, she paid to park near the college dorm and walked onto the campus. She texted Ari and she responded almost immediately. *In class. Meet me in the courtyard in thirty minutes.*

After finding the courtyard, Tasha settled on a bench and pulled her cell phone out of her handbag. She texted Harrison to let him know she had arrived safely. She knew he was in the middle of a busy work day so she had not expected a response from him yet, but she received one. *Good to know you made it safely. I will call you later tonight. I love you.*

Timing

Tasha sat there people watching for the next half hour. College students came in such varieties. There are fresh out of high school students who have a plan to study seriously and pursue a certain career and never look back on that choice. There are kids relishing their freedom from home and parents and partying is the only thing on their minds. Then there are the adults who believed it's never too late to go back to school. Tasha particularly admired those people. *Follow your dreams. Don't see the day when you're out of time to do something you've always wanted to do. Do it now.* Suddenly Tasha was missing the business world and her presence in home design. She never gave that another thought now as she spotted Ari walking in the distance. She was wearing dark-washed jeans, a white v-neck t-shirt with a red college hoodie tied around her waist, and red flip flops on her feet. Tasha smiled to herself as she too unintentionally dressed to blend in on campus, wearing skinny dark-washed jeans, a lime green sweater with a hood and black flip flops. The September air already felt chilly, but there was nothing warmer than the embrace of her daughter as she reached for her.

"Thank you so much for coming, mom." Tasha pulled her daughter out of her arms and looked at her. She was wearing very little makeup, just some mascara and lip gloss and her eyes appeared tired and sad.

"You know I would not be anywhere else," Tasha

told her as they sat down beside each other on the bench Tasha had been waiting on. When Ari told her that she was done with her classes for the day, she asked her mother if she wanted to go somewhere first, maybe to her hotel to check in, or to get something to eat. Tasha responded with certainty, "Talk to me. Here and now. We have all evening for everything else. Sit here and tell me what happened so I can help you feel better."

"Apparently I was born with what Blake calls a silver spoon in my mouth, whatever the hell that means," Ari started to explain. "He hates how I *already* drive *such a nice car* and he said it hurts his pride each time I pay for dinner or something fun that we do together. Mom, I swear, I'm not rubbing anything in his face. I just know he does not have the extra money to always pay. Why can't he understand I'm just trying to help?"

Tasha sighed before speaking. "The two of you have had very different upbringings and sometimes it's too challenging for opposites to mesh." Ari started crying and Tasha reached for her hand. "But that does not mean you both can't bend or change a little to make it work. If you want him, and he wants you, that's all that matters. That alone is worth fighting for."

"He doesn't want me anymore. He's made that very clear, mom."

Timing

"Then let it be. Let him be. He was your first love, and although it does not seem like it right now, there will be another love in your life."

"But he won't be like Blake," Ari whined and Tasha could almost see the little girl in her surface again.

"No, he won't be, but he will be special in his own way and more important than anything, if he wants to be with you, he will accept you for who you are. Never forget love isn't easy. We all have faults and quirks and issues which some people can look past and others cannot. If you really love someone, those things become almost meaningless compared to what is really important."

"This is just all so hard, I don't know if I'm ready for adulthood." Ari was partly teasing and Tasha smiled at her. "Just wait, honey. You've only just begun."

***

Tasha spent two days with Ari. They ate together at a few of their favorite restaurants and they spent many hours talking in Tasha's hotel room at night. Ari was far from being ready to move on without Blake, but she promised her mother she would try. Seeing him in class a few times a week has not made the process of getting over him any easier. Ari told her mom they shared very little small talk and it felt awkward when they tried to communicate. Blake was being very cold toward her, and Ari was extremely hurt. Tasha made sure Ari knew no matter what happens with Blake, it will be for the best. She also reassured her if Blake were to change his mind and want to reunite, it is okay to give someone a second chance. Ari took that advice to heart and then turned the attention on her mother. "You mean like you and dad have given each other a second chance?" she asked, still feeling grateful for how her parents rekindled their love.

"Yeah, just like your dad and I." Tasha thought how it certainly has not been easy and it was about to become even more challenging with the uncertainty that lies ahead.

***

Driving home alone on the long stretches of interstate roads gave Tasha more time to think about her life. She didn't have many regrets, but she carried a few. She now hoped she is teaching her daughter how to fight for what she believes in, to sometimes accept defeat, and when something as you know it ends, always believe a new beginning will bring something better.

So about those regrets, she thought to herself, *can I live with mine?* A huge regret which will always hang over Tasha's head is how she allowed herself to lose sight of the things that truly mattered in her life. Number one being

Timing

her husband. She and Harrison had definitely lost sight of what it takes and what it means to hold a marriage together. Tasha took her own advice, which she had repeatedly given to her daughter the past couple of days, and reminded herself of how she is fighting for her marriage now because she believes in it. This is their new beginning and she is going to have faith that it will bring something better into their lives. And then she thought about the particular regret which has been weighing unbearably heavily on her heart. Walking away from Jack Williams. She knew she didn't belong with him, but she wished more with each passing day she would not have cut him out of her life so harshly. She deeply missed his companionship. Maybe he needed to know that she does not hate him. She hates how the consequences of his actions took her mother away from her, but she couldn't see the reasoning behind dwelling on the hurt any longer.

CHAPTER 20

It was early evening when Tasha pulled into the garage at home. She was looking forward to being with Harrison and Spence again. She shifted her car into park, turned off the ignition and got out to walk around the back of her car to retrieve her bag from the trunk and that is when Harrison barreled out of the house with Spence behind him, both of them looking frantic. "Keep your suitcase in the car," Harrison said as Tasha noticed he had his cell phone held up to his ear. "We have to go back to New York tonight, I'm on the phone with the airport to get the three of us a flight out as soon as possible."

Timing

"What for?" were the only words Tasha managed to speak before Harrison tried to explain. She looked down and saw Spence holding his own suitcase and he had tears in his eyes and panic on his face. "It's Ari, she tried to... she swallowed a bottle of pills, her roommate found her unconscious." Harrison immediately started talking to the operator at the airport who had previously put him on hold. He booked three one-way tickets to New York City in exactly two hours.

Tasha ran through the house throwing more clothes into two additional suitcases for both her and Harrison. Spence was following her around in her bedroom when she asked him for the second time if he had remembered to pack underwear and his toothbrush. Finally, he couldn't take it anymore and he fell apart. "Yes! Stop asking me that. Mom, please, I'm scared and I don't care if I have to wear dirty underwear and never brush my teeth again... I just want my sister to be okay." Tasha grabbed her son by the shoulders and bent down to look him directly into his eyes. "She will be okay. I promise she will." Tasha pulled him close and the two of them cried together. And that is one promise Tasha prayed she could keep.

***

Lori Bell

So many thoughts were racing through Tasha's mind as they sat in silence in the airport awaiting their flight. They had already talked at length while driving to the airport. *Ari seemed fine a few short hours ago, or at least strong enough to get through Blake's breaking up with her. Why in the hell didn't she call me back to her if she was feeling so lost and so desperate? I would have turned around in a heartbeat. Who does something like that? Is our daughter really that unstable?* Every thought, every question, every curse word and every tear occurred in front of Spence. Harrison and Tasha both agreed he is going along to see his sister. He needed to. And he also needed to have his eyes opened to the fact that life is not perfect, real problems surface and people deal with them. The right way. *Did Ari really think suicide was the answer?* Tasha felt half out of her mind trying to process what her daughter had attempted to do. *She tried to take her own life.*

***

Tasha didn't even remember the flight to New York City or the ride in the taxi to the hospital. It was well past visiting hours, but the nurses were expecting them. Spence walked alongside of his parents and one of the nurses offered to take him to have a snack or a soda in the lounge. Tasha agreed, but told him he should come right back, and then she and Harrison listened to what another nurse had to tell them.

Timing

Ari had consumed an entire bottle of Extra-Strength Tylenol. Harrison was immediately relieved to hear she had not taken any illegal drugs. On top of the obvious problem, the last thing he believed his daughter needed is to be in trouble with the law. Thinking like a lawyer kept him from falling apart like any father has undoubtedly felt like doing in his current situation.

Tasha and Harrison learned how a suicide attempt with Tylenol is painful, and includes an aftermath of nausea, vomiting, diarrhea, and irritability symptoms. In more serious cases where the Tylenol's active ingredient acetaminophen is in a person's system for a longer period of time, it affects the liver and can cause the liver to fail. The nurse informed them an ambulance was called to the campus soon after Ari had lost consciousness. The Tylenol had interfered with Ari's natural body process of breathing and circulation and her stomach was pumped and emptied immediately upon her emergency arrival at the hospital to prevent any further, more serious damage.

The nurse informed them of how no additional lab tests have been ordered for Ari, but a psychiatric evaluation must be completed at the hospital before her release in a day or two. Tasha winced at the thought of her daughter being labeled as *unstable*, or *crazy*. All she wanted to do now was see her. Get to her. Run to her.

"I want to see my daughter, please," Tasha said

cutting short the nurse's next words. By now Spence rejoined them and all three of them followed the nurse into a dim-lit hospital room. There were two beds in the room, one empty and one with Ari lying in it. She was sleeping but the stillness of her body this one time sent chills throughout Tasha. Her daughter could have died. She could have been successful at taking her own life. *Killing herself.*

She looked pale, but peaceful and Tasha wondered how it could be possible for her daughter to go so quickly from holding it together to falling apart. She had just left her hours earlier. *What could have happened in those hours to make Ari feel so lost, helpless, hopeless?*

"She was very sick earlier," the nurse spoke to them as they all three looked forlorn at the sight of Ari lying in a hospital bed. "The doctor will speak to you when he is available tonight or tomorrow, but you should know we believe the worst is over for her in terms of the retching." *The worst is over?* Tasha hoped that were true in every sense. She wanted her daughter back, a young woman who she always believed has so much promise, who will not only survive life's challenges but thrive.

***

The next morning Tasha was still awake, sitting in the armchair beside Ari's hospital bed. She had asked

Timing

Harrison to check into a hotel near the hospital so he and Spence could get some sleep, but she wanted to stay and be there when their daughter woke up. Harrison said they would be back first thing in the morning, but told her to call him if she needed him for any reason. His support through this had amazed Tasha. She knew the extent of his hurt and his anger, because she was feeling every bit of it too, but she was gaining strength from his actions and his words. *Their family will survive this.*

When Ari opened her eyes and saw her mom beside her, she cried. She felt obvious shame for what she did to herself, and to her family. Tasha stood up from the chair she had been sitting in almost all night long and she sat down on the bed beside her daughter, holding her and rocking her as she sobbed in her arms. "It's going to be alright," Tasha said to her when she finally calmed down.

"That is what you told me before you left," Ari began to explain, "and I believed you. I really thought it is what it is, and I can get through this. But then I went to class and on my way there, I saw him. He was in the courtyard and he was kissing his new girlfriend. I didn't know there is someone else. He criticized me for all of my faults and accused me of being the reason he wanted out, but really it was him wanting someone else." Tasha listened with wide eyes and then she asked her daughter, "Did you confront him?"

"Yes, I rudely interrupted him sticking his tongue down *her* throat," Ari began to tear up again and it was at that moment when Tasha realized it was going to take a very long time for her daughter to get over her first love. She isn't just heartbroken. Her actions have proved she *is* unstable. No matter how much pain her boyfriend had caused her, she should have taken care of herself, carried on, and not given up on her entire life so quickly. Ari is in quicksand and Tasha felt terrified for her. "He told me to move on, let it be, and then he walked away with her. Just knowing he's with her, touching her…"

"Stop it! Stop doing this to yourself, Ari. You cannot torture yourself like this. No one is worth what you tried to do tonight. Do you hear me? No one!" Tasha raised her voice and immediately stopped herself from saying anything more. It would be wrong to tell Ari how she is being *selfish* or *stupid* because some people are fragile and can so easily reach the edge. It's a sickness to find oneself in such a dark place and Tasha vowed right then and there to help her daughter heal. "Your dad and I are going to get you the help you need. I obviously have not gotten through to you, you may hear my words but you are not truly listening. You're not going to be given a choice, you have to see a psychiatrist before you are discharged from this hospital. So, please, let a professional help. And let me love you and be here for you no matter what you are thinking or feeling. Just reach out to me. I'm

Timing

begging you never to give up like that again." Tasha had tears streaming down her face as she embraced her daughter again, lying side by side with her in that hospital bed.

***

When Harrison and Spence returned to the hospital, Tasha met them in the hallway to privately talk. She told them Ari is no longer sick from the overdose but she is irritable and weepy at times. Tasha then asked Harrison and Spence to walk into her hospital room with a positive attitude and with the intent to cheer her. She specifically told them not to bring up Ari's suicide attempt, unless Ari initiates. That is not what she needs from her father or her brother right now. She needs to know she is loved and she also needs to get her mind off of being sad. Harrison and Spence agreed they will do their best to make Ari laugh as Tasha excused herself to make a phone call and told them she would be back shortly.

As they entered Ari's room, Tasha walked down the hallway and into an empty lounge. She sat down and scrolled through the list of contacts in her cell phone and she stopped when she found Kelsey's name. She still had her logged under Kelsey Newman, her married name when they were neighbors in New York City before

Kelsey's husband died. And also before the Wheelans moved to Baltimore. Tasha did not hesitate. She just called her.

Kelsey answered immediately. "Hey, old friend!"

"Hey yourself," Tasha said, as she began to explain what she needed from Kelsey. "There's been an emergency and I'm back in New York City and I desperately need your help." Tasha proceeded to explain to a shocked Kelsey what Ari had done and how worried she now is about what will happen to her. Tasha told Kelsey how she specifically remembers a particular psychiatrist pushing Kelsey through her pain when she lost her husband, Kyle. Tasha stressed how she does not want *some shrink stamping a crazy label on her child as a routine part of the job.* She wants someone who *truly cares about her patients, and who will be successful at helping her daughter come out of this awful trench.*

"Say no more. Her name is Dr. Judy Winthrop, her practice is at Laneview Hospital," Kelsey informed her, not knowing Laneview Hospital is exactly where Ari had been admitted. "I promise you, she will reach Ari and put her on a very healthy path to complete healing."

That is exactly what Tasha needed to hear. She repeatedly thanked Kelsey for being there for her, and especially for giving her this hope. Hope by the name of

Timing

Dr. Judy Winthrop. This didn't feel like a long shot to Tasha. This felt like an answered prayer.

CHAPTER 21

A woman, who appeared to be in her mid-sixties, was dressed to the nines under her white lab coat in a pale pink wrap blouse, black flared-leg dress pants and black patent ballet flats as she approached both Tasha and Ari in the waiting room outside of her office. Kelsey Reiss had made that urgent phone call for Tasha. She told Dr. Judy about her former neighbor's daughter and requested her help. Dr. Judy reviewed Ari Wheelan's file from her visit to the emergency room and current two-night stay at the hospital. The continued length of her hospital stay now depended upon her psychiatric evaluation today.

Timing

After introducing herself and shaking both of their hands, Dr. Judy asked Tasha to join them for the first few minutes of Ari's session. They both stood up and followed her into her office. The office smelled nice, like vanilla, as Tasha noticed a small candle burning on a low table in front of the sofa. It was as if they were being welcomed into someone's living room, maybe even a friend's. Tasha observed Dr. Judy as she asked them to sit down. Nearly the exact same height as Tasha, the psychiatrist wore her cropped jet black hair spiked all over her head. Her facial features behind her dark-rimmed glasses were striking and perfectly accented with makeup. Despite twenty-five or thirty extra pounds, Tasha saw this woman in front of her as striking. Now she just hoped for Dr. Judy to be the amazing therapist she has heard about.

The psychiatrist's first question for Ari was direct. She had not held back. She looked at Ari and asked, "So your life, in your mind, was bad enough for you to want to end it?" Tasha's eyes widened when she heard the question for her daughter and she, like Dr. Judy, awaited an answer.

"No, I mean yes. I really felt like I didn't have anything left to live for," Ari admitted, sounding young and selfish.

"What about your parents and your little brother? You don't think they love you? You don't believe they would not have missed you and grieved for you for the rest of their lives if you had been successful at overdosing on pills?" Ari looked uncomfortable and Tasha did not know what to think about this therapist. *Was this some form of a tough psychiatry?* "I know what I did was wrong. I saw my mom's face when I woke up in the hospital and I am still seeing how my dad is avoiding the subject of *what I did* because it hurts too much to go there. And, I know what kind of a scare I put into my little brother."

"So you understand that you are loved by your family and they want to see you through your struggle with losing your first boyfriend?" Dr. Judy seemed to soften a bit when she finished her sentence. Everyone understands heartbreak because almost everyone has been there, Tasha was thinking to herself as she continued to listen during this session and she wondered how long Dr. Judy would allow her to stay in the room.

"Yes, I understand how they want to help but it feels like I can't be helped because this can't be fixed," Ari admitted. "I don't know how to go to school and be a college student here without thinking every second of every day how much I miss Blake."

"It's going to take time, and you have to allow yourself that time to let these feelings lessen and finally pass. There will come a day when you won't see this break-up as the end of the world." Dr. Judy's words made

Timing

perfect sense to Tasha, and Ari wanted to believe that will happen for her, eventually, but she is just nowhere near there yet. Not in her mind, nor in her heart. "You said that you don't know how to resume your life here, in school. Maybe you should consider going back home with your parents. Consider enrolling in a college in Baltimore, or taking the rest of the semester off to regroup."

"Wouldn't that be running away?" Ari asked her, and Tasha was surprised at how mature she suddenly sounded again. The person who has been so lost the past few days seemed to be in search of finding her strength again. Or so Tasha had hoped, with all of her heart.

"It's only running away if you do not face your feelings. I think getting away from seeing your former boyfriend on a daily basis would do you a world of good. You may be feeling embarrassed or ashamed and sometimes it's good to face that and hold your head up high, but in some cases you just need to walk away and begin again. Leave that young man where he belongs, in the dust. Do not give him the privilege of ever seeing your beautiful face again." Dr. Judy smiled widely, her teeth so perfectly aligned and bright white, and Ari returned a genuine smile to her as Tasha looked at them and interrupted. "Can I say something, please?" Dr. Judy nodded her head, yes. "You really believe it would be best for Ari to pack up and go home, for good?"

"I believe your daughter needs time and space and a lot of attention. I do not know if leaving her college of choice in New York City *for good* is the answer. Time will tell. If you choose to return, then so be it. If you choose to switch directions in order to move on, then I say that is wonderful. Just find a way to cope with this struggle which has brought you to your knees. Do not feed the pain, just get around it, get past it any way you can."

"You're moving back home!" Tasha exclaimed and both Dr. Judy and Ari turned their heads to look at her. Her excitement overwhelmed them both and Tasha's face flushed.

"No. That is a decision your daughter will have to make for herself," Dr. Judy responded matter-of-factly. "Now, it's time for Ari and I to talk privately." Tasha had her cue to leave and she did so without hesitation. She, herself, felt rejuvenated. Her daughter is coming home and that could not have felt more reassuring to her.

***

Well it wasn't that easy. Forty-five minutes later, Ari walked out of her session alone and informed her mother she is not leaving New York City, she wanted to stay in college there, and she is not ready to never see Blake again. Tasha felt her jaw drop and her eyes widen as her nineteen-year-old daughter stood before her insisting she should stay in a place where she obviously felt like the world was caving in around her. Tasha felt extremely concerned, but before she panicked she told Ari to sit down in the waiting room and she left her there when she knocked once on Dr. Judy's office door, opened it, and walked in. She closed the door behind her as the psychiatrist looked up and over her dark-rimmed glasses at Tasha as she remained seated in the large leather cushioned chair behind her desk.

"What just happened in here? When I left you with her, she was going to move back home, which was *your* idea, and now she's adamant about staying?" Tasha was unnerved. *What kind of therapist is the woman anyway?* She obviously had made a mistake choosing her to take care of Ari.

"No, I merely suggested she walk away from her problems, run if she needed to...." Dr. Judy's response sounded as if she was about to wink and Tasha instantly understood.

"I'm not a shrink, but I think I know what you just did. You used reverse psychology, didn't you? You wanted Ari to choose, on her own, to stay here to face her problems and what she did. I'm not so sure I agree because I don't think Ari is strong enough to handle that feat right now."

"She isn't. Not right now, but she will be." Dr. Judy said with confidence. "Your daughter, like all of us at various points in our lives, needs to learn how to own up to her actions. Yes, she could run back home and hide in the safety of your arms but what would that do to her in the long run? It would eat her alive. We dwell when we are not productive. Here, she will be productive studying and hopefully getting back into the land of the living with her friends."

"And what about Blake? What if she cannot handle being around him, seeing him with his new girlfriend or just being on the receiving end of his coldness?" Tasha had reached the beyond worried point.

"I will be requiring her to see me three times a week for the next month. If I see she is not benefitting from staying here, I will suggest for you and your husband to step in and make her come home. You, of course, may decide that for her right now but I don't recommend making her feel forced into anything." Dr. Judy then all but swore to Tasha how she knows what she is doing as an experienced therapist with more than thirty years in practice. "I will try to reassure you by telling you how I have seen much worse in teenagers who have attempted suicide. Your daughter reacted severely in the moment and afterward she has shown incredible remorse. Most teens are not sorry they attempted, they are just

Timing

sorry it didn't work and are already planning a second attempt. That is not Ari. With the proper therapy and by giving her the free-will to continue her life here, I honestly believe she will make it through this just fine."

Tasha was not convinced, but she did nod her head in agreement with Dr. Judy and sincerely thanked her for her help. This wasn't how she imagined the session would go, but this entire nightmare wasn't what she ever would have imagined either for her daughter's first year of college.

***

Two weeks went by and Tasha spent the entire time in New York City hovering over her daughter. Harrison and Spence had flown back to Baltimore and Tasha promised to come home as soon as she knew Ari had found her strength again and could be trusted. She returned to school immediately after her three-day hospital stay and she continued to receive counseling from Dr. Judy a few days a week. Now, it was time for Tasha to meet with the psychiatrist. She requested the meeting with the doctor after telling her on the phone how it's been two weeks and she still feels as if she is searching for some kind of sign with Ari. Maybe a red flag that she is on her way off the deep end again? Or, maybe she just needed the reassurance. She wanted to see her daughter move on with her college life, and Tasha wanted to resume hers back in Baltimore.

Tasha walked in Dr. Judy's office alone. After her phone call, Dr. Judy agreed to see Tasha, to talk to her about her daughter's progress. Or lack thereof.

"Please, come in, Mrs. Wheelan." Dr. Judy looked beautiful again to Tasha and she smiled at her as Tasha sat down with her on the couch. She was not there as a patient, their conversation was not being recorded or analyzed. Tasha felt comfortable there, but worried. And Dr. Judy recognized that. "So you're life has been on hold for weeks and you need to know if and when you can leave your daughter. What does your heart tell you?"

"I know my daughter is struggling, but I also know she has what it takes to move past her pain. What I don't know is what will happen when I leave New York. I hope to God she isn't just pretending with me." Tasha was being completely honest.

"Why do you say pretending?" Dr. Judy interrupted.

"I don't know, I really can't put my finger on it for sure but I feel like Ari is keeping something from me. I feel like she is telling me she is fine just so I will leave her alone." Tasha sighed and Dr. Judy nodded her head yes, repeatedly, as if she were in total agreement with her.

Timing

"She most definitely is a master at telling people what they want to hear," Dr. Judy said and Tasha suddenly wanted to defend her daughter, but she remained silent and allowed her to finish. "It took me almost the entire first week of therapy to get her to just be real, to tell me what she is feeling instead of agreeing with me and, like you said, telling me what she thought I wanted to hear."

"So have you been able to get her to open up?" Tasha asked.

"Yes I have. I told her I was not going to allow her to waste my time and hers. I asked her to find another therapist and that is when she broke down and really spoke to me about her feelings."

Tasha immediately wanted to hear more. "Is that why you agreed to see me today? Are you going to fill in the blanks for me? What is she hiding?"

"I cannot break that confidentiality," she answered, "but I can tell you that your concerns are warranted. Your daughter is dealing with a lot of unspoken emotions. Go to her, talk to her, really talk to her. You are her mother, she adores you and above all else she does not want to disappoint you."

Tasha felt teary and her hands were trembling. She knew Dr. Judy could not share any specific details, but what she had told her frightened her. *Was Ari going to be okay?* Tasha expressed her appreciation to the doctor and left her office.

***

She went directly to Ari's dorm room and caught her leaving. "Mom! I told you I'm in class today until four. We can do something after that," Ari stated, sounding annoyed while standing in the doorway of her dorm room with her backpack slung over one shoulder and her hand on the door knob and she appeared to be trying to inch the door closed as Tasha stood in front of her.

"Skip it," Tasha said, nudging her daughter through the doorway and back into the room. And that is when she saw him sitting on her bed with his shirt off, his jeans unbuttoned, and he was barefoot. Blake was back.

"What the…?" Tasha looked at him and then back at Ari. "Do either of you mind telling me what it going on here, um, besides the obvious?" Tasha's face flushed and she tried not to stare at her daughter's boyfriend. *Or, ex-boyfriend.*

"I will explain, mom," Ari said, looking and sounding frazzled as Blake grabbed his t-shirt and immediately pulled it over his head after he zipped and buttoned his jeans. "Blake and I are back together."

Timing

"For good this time," he added, looking at Tasha and then walking over to take Ari's hand in his and she smiled at him. The two of them were almost the same height and did make a striking couple, but Tasha halted herself from admiring anything about the fact that they are a couple again.

"Blake, I would like to speak to my daughter alone." Tasha had never met him before and didn't want a formal introduction now because it was taking everything inside of her, everything she had, to not take another step closer to this young man and put her hands on his neck and strangle him. He is the reason her daughter has become someone whom she does not recognize. Fragile. Unstable. And then Tasha thought, submissive. She did not like the way her daughter seemed at this boy's mercy. What he says goes. What he wants, he gets. Tasha was growing angrier with each passing second as she watched him slip on his tennis shoes, grab his backpack from off of the chair by the door and then turn around and walk back toward her daughter. He didn't kiss her, but he got close to her face and whispered, *call me later*. And then he left the dorm room. Tasha and Ari were now alone to talk, and Tasha intended to get some answers.

"You've taken him back? Since when? I've been here for two weeks, watching you practically day and night, and now I walk in here to find him half naked with you?" Tasha tried not to raise her voice, but she felt so angry and it was evident.

"Since right after I got out of the hospital. I saw him in class, we talked over coffee afterward, and he told me he wants me back," Ari explained.

"And you took him back, just like that?" Tasha was fuming. "Don't you see that he could hurt you all over again? And what then? Will you not being able to handle losing him and succeed at killing yourself next time?"

"Mom! No! Don't say that. I know what I did was wrong and I swear to you I will never do anything like that again." Ari immediately had tears streaming down her face. "I love him and I need him. I knew you would shit a brick if you found out, so I kept it from you."

"So now I have to worry about you lying to me?" Tasha almost spat the words at her. "What else, Ari? What else are you hiding?"

"Nothing. I just want to get my life back with him. I'm not whole without him," Ari confessed.

"Don't Ari. Don't believe that. You are a wonderful, amazing young woman. You can be complete without him. I understand what love feels like, I know what happens to a mind and a heart when you find someone you want to spend the rest of your life with. I also know

Timing

what it feels like to disconnect from that person. It hurts, but you can survive without him."

"How would you know?" Ari asked her mother.

"What?" Tasha replied.

"I am simply saying how the hell would you know that you could survive alone? You never left dad when he broke your heart. You hung in there, you stayed, and after a really long time you pushed, you shoved, and you fought your way back to him. And it worked. It took years, but you didn't give up and you got dad back and everything is good again."

Tasha could not believe what she heard. *Oh dear Lord, my daughter has watched and learned from me. I've hardly led by example.* "How can you even compare our situations? We are talking about a marriage that spans two decades and a first love. You've only dated him for a matter of months," Tasha stated. "Forget about me and what you have watched me do. What are you doing, Ari? What are you thinking?"

"I think you need to understand that I love him," Ari stated.

"I do understand, and I would support you one hundred percent if I didn't see how unhealthy this relationship is for you." Tasha walked toward her daughter and reached for her. Ari responded by taking both of her mother's hands into her own.

"Mom, it's time for you to go back home. Dad and Spence need you. I am going to be okay, and I swear to you if I ever feel like I'm not on a good path, I will reach out to you. But, please, just let me make my own choices. Don't doubt me forever for one stupid mistake," Ari sounded so incredibly sensible at that moment and Tasha found herself caving. *What other choice did she have?* Life works that way sometimes. You do all you can possibly do and then you take a step back and breathe and believe everything will work out. Tasha cried as she held her daughter close and managed to speak the words, "Call me, daily. I mean it. Keep me updated on everything that is going on. I will be here in record time if you ever need me."

CHAPTER 22

Tasha resumed her life in Baltimore with her husband and son. It was not easy for her to be so far away from Ari again, but between her and Harrison they regularly checked on their daughter and felt great relief to mutually agree she sounded happy, and like her old self again.

During the holiday season, Ari took advantage of the month-long break from her classes and she came home to be with her family. That is when Tasha found herself completely convinced her daughter had crossed over that once unsteady bridge in her life, and survived. It also may have taken burning that bridge to be able to move on, and Tasha admired her daughter for the measures she finally ended up taking in order to grab a hold of her life and continue on. Ari showed up at the airport in Baltimore two days before Christmas. And she wasn't alone.

From a distance in the crowd at the baggage claim, Tasha saw Ari with a young man at her side. She immediately assumed it was Blake, although her daughter had never mentioned any plans to bring him home with her for the holiday break. Tasha had been walking through the airport with both Harrison and Spence and when she spotted Ari she said aloud to them, "She has Blake with her." She instantly had to tell herself not to let his presence dampen their holiday together as a family if it was Ari's choice to have him there. As she stepped closer and Harrison focused on his daughter as well, he said to his wife just as she also realized, "That is not Blake."

***

Turns out Ari found a new boyfriend, twenty-two years old and a college senior. Ari will soon turn twenty and Tasha liked the fact that she is seeing someone a little bit older. That would not have been acceptable in high school, but it somehow worked for Tasha now. Nathan Seeley, six-foot two with jet black thick hair and a solid but fit build, reminded Tasha of a man she met twenty years ago. Her husband. It was not as if Nathan and Harrison actually looked alike other than their hair color, but Tasha thought of it as uncanny the way the two of them were so similar, especially having the same views about life. Nathan saw the world as his for taking, as Harrison always has. He was about to earn a business degree and he was in search of a job that would earn him millions. Again, for Tasha, she was seeing so much of a young Harrison in Nathan. Big dreams and big ambition to match. Ari was taken with him and they complimented each other in the best ways, but she did not appear to be overly smitten or clingy, which Tasha was incredibly relieved to see. The two of them have been dating for two months, Ari informed her mother late one night while the boys were outside in the backyard under the lights, bundled up for a game of touch football.

Ari explained to her mother how she had not told her or her father about Nathan because she wanted to see where this new adventure took her, to see if it was even serious after their first couple of dates. She wanted to take this relationship slow and just enjoy his company. Ari told her mother she does not know if she is *in love* with him, but she certainly loves spending time with him and getting to know him. Bringing him home to meet her parents and her brother had not meant they were serious, Ari stated to her mother, it only meant they wanted to spend more time together before school resumes. Tasha didn't pry about Nathan or his family, she just allowed Ari to tell her as much as she felt comfortable. But she did ask her what happened with Blake.

With sadness in her eyes, Ari explained why Blake was not *the one* for her. She told her mother how she didn't know if she ever would again feel her heart race when another man walks into a room and all he had to do was look at her and she would instantly feel special and desired. Ari caught Blake cheating on her and this time she walked away. The hardest thing she has had to do thus far in her life was to close the door on him, literally the time when he showed up at her dorm room door apologizing and begging for another chance.

Tasha has never been more proud of her daughter, and she told her so. It took abundant courage for Ari to get out of an unhealthy relationship and Tasha admired her for all she has endured and for how she has obviously become stronger because of it. A young man like Blake could have continued to form Ari to be weak and compliant, had she allowed him to. Instead, Ari chose to move on. Without him.

***

It was early January when Tasha was driving from Harrison's office. He had called her because he left a file at home on the nightstand beside their bed and he needed it. Tasha had been planning to make a trip downtown anyway, so she stopped in at the law firm to deliver it to him. When she was leaving she heard a loud diesel motor and saw a black truck drive by the parking lot, and she instantly thought of Jack Williams. She could not see the driver or the license plates, but she wondered if it was him.

Tasha had been to the cemetery three times since that day when she saw him last, once in the fall and twice throughout the cold winter. She visited her mother's grave each time, but never attempted to drive up to the house on the hill. She convinced herself to leave it up to fate like she had all of those other times when she drove into the cemetery, parked her car, and he would just appear. That

Timing

never happened any of those times, and while she always left disappointed she refused to make anything happen between them. Today, however, she felt compelled. Drawn. She needed to go there. She no longer carried any anger toward him, and he needed to know that. It's time she told him.

As Tasha drove on the outskirts of the city, she wondered if she was making a mistake. Would her presence lead Jack on in any way? That was not her intention. She was not looking for a relationship with him, she had even gotten past missing his companionship every second of every day. Tasha wondered if she is feeling emotional because Sarah Loft is nearing the end of her pregnancy. It is January and her baby is due next month. Tasha had again pressed Harrison about telling her as soon as he receives the news and for him to be tested immediately. She no longer wanted to leave Harrison, and she told him so, but accepting his child into their lives is going to be a lot for her and their children to handle. Harrison, again, was adamant to *move on because this baby is not going to be his.*

Tasha drove faster, feeling an emotional pull to the cemetery grounds. To Jack. She missed their conversations. She missed how he reached her soul. She missed how he listened, offered advice, and sometimes just held her. Tasha loves Harrison with her entire heart and their life together is good and they are both working harder to keep it that way. But, Harrison has his flaws. Maybe it is just, in general, a male flaw but listening is not Harrison's strongest quality. Jack, however, has that quality in spades and Tasha thought of it as his strongest character trait. Harrison could sometimes be distant or even seem uncaring when Tasha wanted to have one of those conversations, a conversation where two people completely connect, speaking and listening. Like she used to experience with Jack. He knew her soul.

Tasha had no intention of having an affair, of even believing she *belonged* with Jack. She wondered if maybe they are soul mates, in the sense where they are just meant to be there for each other to lift each other up and have fun together. To be bonded as friends.

It has been four months since she saw him last, but right now the time just felt right to go to him as Tasha drove into the cemetery grounds and up to the house on the hill. There had been a light snowfall overnight and some of the one-inch white covering was still visible in the grass, around the graves. When Tasha reached his house, she saw his truck on the driveway and she heard it running. She thought how it must have been him driving downtown. She shut off the engine to her car and got out. When she was walking alongside of his truck, she noticed it full of cardboard boxes in the back. She didn't look closer, she just kept walking toward the door. She thought of taking off her boots when he invited her inside again. She felt cozy today wearing an off-white cowlneck sweater with a dark brown down coat that ended well past her waist, and her dark-washed skinny jeans with knee-high brown leather boots. The soles were flat but grippy enough in case the sidewalks were slippery when she went out to run errands earlier. Tasha knocked twice and waited. It took what seemed like an eternity before Tasha heard footsteps approaching the door on the inside. *Maybe she is just anxious to see him again.*

When the door opened, it was not Jack standing there. It was Brooklyn. Her hair, still as Tasha remembered from their one-time meeting, looked poker-straight, dark and stringy, hanging well past her shoulders and down to the middle of her back. She looked too thin in her tight black jeans, worn black boots, a white tank top and a men's red plaid shirt thrown over it. Her breasts were fake and visible in her tank top as Tasha looked up and suddenly felt ridiculous for being at Jack's door. He had taken *her* back. He went back to his brother's life, the life he swore he could not handle anymore. Maybe he did it for the girls? *Maybe I broke his heart and pushed him back into her arms, back to Texas?* Brooklyn interrupted Tasha's racing thoughts when she spoke first. "I was just on my way out with the last of Jack's things," she said to Tasha.

Tasha felt her face flush. "So he's moving back to Texas with you?" *Damn her, all she will do is make him miserable again.* "Um, I am a friend of Jack's and I just came to–"

"It's a little late to pay your respects, which is what I believe you said you were doing for Jackson Senior the last time I came here," Brooklyn said as Tasha realized she did remember her. But Tasha didn't understand her comment.

"I'm sorry, what? Is Jack here? I just need a minute of his time–"

"His time was up six weeks ago," Brooklyn's words were harsh, but she began to soften as she explained. "I don't even remember your name, but it's obvious to me that you cared about Jack so I am going to be the bearer of some really sad news. Jack died unexpectedly at the end of November. Shocked the hell out of all of us back home. The autopsy results showed he had a heart condition, a defect, probably from birth. It was never detected, you know like some of those young athletes you hear about on the local news…" She was speaking as if she were talking about the weather, an unexpected blizzard that was only supposed to amount to a couple of inches of snow. Tasha was dumbfounded. She stopped listening to Brooklyn's ramble, which sounded uneducated at times, and interrupted her. "Oh my God, stop saying those things. Why would you make up a lie like that? To hurt me? Do you want to hurt me? If you think I want Jack, you're wrong. He is my friend and I'm just here to talk to him. I want to see him. I know you are on your way back to Texas and he's moving there too I assume. If that is his decision then so be it, but I do at the very least want to say goodbye to him."

"He's gone, lady. Dead. He's not going to be mine, yours, or anyone else's ever again." Brooklyn's words were harsh, but Tasha heard her this time. She registered the facts and began to feel the pain. The loss. And she wanted to cry and scream and curse the unspeakable timing of this.

Timing

"I …can't…believe…it," Tasha tried to speak, but not much else was coming out.

"I know, and I'm sorry, if that means anything coming from me," Brooklyn said, actually sounding sincere. "The house will be up for sale soon. I am not handling it, Jack's uncle will be back and forth to manage that. I just came back to collect some of his things and bring them to his mother. I was going to sell the truck, because he willed so much else to my girls, but I think I want to hang onto it for awhile and drive it back to Texas just to feel like he's close still." Tasha did not want to hear anymore. This woman continued to take advantage of Jack, even now. Even in death. "You know, you can take a look around inside if there is anything you want. I mean, I know how much he cared about you and you obviously are in shock here. I am gonna leave, so you can just sit down or something." Brooklyn's voice was ringing in Tasha's ears as she backed away from the door and spoke, attempting to leave, hoping she could trust her feet to move and her legs to hold her up. She felt her insides crumbling. This was not just a shock to her system. This is heartbreak at its best. This is a part of her soul that perished and would now be gone forever.

Tasha did not even know for sure what she said to Brooklyn as she turned to leave, she couldn't even hear herself speak, much less comprehend any of it. She practically fell back into her car, turned the ignition and shifted into reverse. All the while, she was staring at his truck. Hearing the engine run loudly, she was imagining Jack behind the wheel. His smile, sometimes it looked like more of a smirk, and it always made Tasha instantly happy. Happy to see him. But, now, she would never see him again. *Oh dear God, no…no…no!*

CHAPTER 23

Driving away, her mind was racing, she felt panicked and her thoughts were unbearably sad. *Jack is really gone? I will never be able to see him, talk to him ever again. Did he know I didn't blame him anymore? How could he? I never told him and now the chance to tell him is gone forever. Along with him.* Tasha's windshield began fogging up. She had forgotten to turn on the defrost switch, in fact she had not even heated the car as she drove away. She felt so cold and any amount of heat blowing out of those car vents would not warm her now. *I lost Jack. The world lost a wonderful, caring, amazing man too young and too soon. Thirty-six years old and he's dead.*

Tasha could feel the tears welling up in her eyes as she continued to drive. She had driven that frontage road numerous times, it was the same road her mother had been driving when Jack crossed the center line in his truck and killed her. She was not thinking about that now. All she could dwell on is *Jack is gone*. "Oh Jack, no, no, no! This is not happening," Tasha words were loud and desperate as she drove alone. Her car was inching its way off the shoulder of the road as she cried and screamed and choked on her sobs at times. She suddenly heard her tires rubbing on the rumble strips of the road's shoulder alerting her to the fact that she is veering off the road. The tactile vibration alarmed her and she was quick to steer her car back onto the highway and between the lines where she again centered her car as she drove. The rear window in her car began to fog up too as Tasha looked into her rearview mirror and noticed she is driving that road alone at the moment. There were no oncoming cars and no one was behind her. She is alone on the road, and feeling pretty damn alone in life at the moment too. Jack died and she never knew it, never heard it, never read it in the newspaper. Never had the chance to say goodbye. She wondered what he was doing at the time his heart gave out. Had he been in pain for awhile and too stubborn to see a doctor? She recalled him complaining about his father being hesitant in that way, maybe he was as well. *Was.* Tasha was thinking of Jack in the past tense. Tears continued to pour out of her eyes and down her face.

Timing

"I forgive you, you know that now, right? What are you doing dying on me? Doesn't God know how much I need you? I hope you knew. Why did I waste so much time? You were so special to me and I cared so damn much…"

Tasha's car was crossing the line but she didn't realize it. She was caught up in her grief. Her vision was blurred with tears and the fogged car windows were now near impossible to see through. She was pounding her hands on the steering wheel and accelerating at the same time. She was angry, utterly devastated, and she was crossing the center line on the highway. And that is when she thought she saw two headlights coming directly at her. The road had curved and her car moved square into the opposite lane of oncoming traffic. She came to her senses at the very last possible second. She saw the car in front of her, and found herself directly in its path. Head on. Tasha gripped the steering wheel harder with both of her hands and she instantly jerked her car to the right and out of the wrong lane. She slammed her foot down firm on the brake pedal, her tires were squealing and it seemed like an eternity before she was able to bring her car to a complete stop. She had managed to guide it over to the shoulder of the road and completely halt it. She sat there trying to inhale through her nose, then attempting to take a deep breath through her mouth. Her hands were shaking and she could hear her own heartbeat pounding inside of her ears. Her face was wet with tears and her hair was matted to her forehead and around her temples. She had jolted herself around pretty crazily behind the steering wheel. Thank goodness she had remembered to buckle her seatbelt, because otherwise she had been oblivious to how to keep herself, and others, safe on the road. *Others*. Tasha immediately looked up and into her rearview mirror. She could see something, but she was not sure what she was looking at. There was no traffic on the road as she opened her car door to get out. The cold, brisk winter air struck her in the face as she looked a ways down the road and spotted a stopped a car, turned onto its side. It only took her a split second to realize she had caused that to happen. She was in the path of *that* car, and someone could be hurt because of her.

Tasha tried to hurry, but the road felt slick under her boots, still from the overnight snowfall which had brought a couple inches in spots but mostly all of it had melted in the daylight. Watching for cars on the road, she managed to pick up her pace and run to the crashed vehicle. As she reached it, she saw two tires up in the air spinning, and she could hear someone moaning or crying. Tasha stood up on her toes to look into the driver's side window and she pounded on it with her fists. "Are you okay?" She yelled through the glass, looking for the driver. She could hear a woman hysterically repeating something that Tasha could not make out the words for. Tasha tugged on the door handle but could not open it because it was locked from the inside. She reached into her coat pocket, relieved to retrieve her cell phone, and she dialed 911. In her panicked state, she had not thought to

Timing

call for help earlier, she kept thinking someone else would drive upon this accident, or hoping the other driver would walk away from this unharmed as she did.

"There's been an accident, on Banter Frontage Road, right at the bend." *Oh dear God, the bend, the frontage road, the site where my mother died after Jack crossed the center line. Is this some kind of sick joke? What are the chances of this happening again and here? And, to me!* She quickly informed the emergency dispatcher of how she could not get the driver's side door open to help the person out of the car. Tasha was told not to move the accident victim. Not under any circumstances. An ambulance is on its way.

She looked directly into the car window again and this time she saw the broken windshield. There wasn't much left intact at all. The break was certainly large enough for a person to fit through. *Oh my God...*

She saw a woman lying on the ground about twenty feet north of the vehicle. Her cries had not appeared to sound far away or muffled because she was trapped inside of the vehicle, but because the woman was a considerable distance away from the car she had been thrown out of. Tasha immediately ran to her, with her feet slipping out from under her again on the slick road surface and the cold wind in her face was showing no mercy. When she reached her, she dropped to her knees. The woman was lying flat on her back and there was blood everywhere. Her face was covered in it, and her long dark hair was matted from it. Tasha felt sheer panic, she had never witnessed anything like this before. She forced herself to remain calm and look at the woman's body lying on the ground pooled in so much blood. *What am I going to do? Where is that damn ambulance?* With hope of keeping her conscious, Tasha started to talk to her, "I am so sorry. Oh gosh, help is on the way, you are going to be fine," but as she did her eyes widened. The woman was wearing a long, dark gray, lined trench coat and she appeared heavyset. It's winter and it's freezing outside. Everyone wore bulky coats in the wintertime. But this coat, however, covered the body of what Tasha recognized as a pregnant woman. And she recognized *her* as Sarah Loft.

Her voice was becoming weaker and she now appeared to be slipping in and out of consciousness as she desperately tried to speak. Then, the next words she spoke and Tasha so clearly heard were, "My…baby…please…save…my…baby."

CHAPTER 24

Tasha watched the ambulance personnel do their job. They asked her numerous questions and she couldn't bring herself to tell them or the police officer on the scene how she caused this accident. She only said she was *driving by and came upon the car, already off the road and the woman hurt on the ground.* When, really, she is the reason this pregnant woman ran off of the road, hit the guard rail and the impact from the crash resulted in her being thrown out of her car. Tasha was not at fault for Sarah Loft not wearing a seatbelt, but she is to blame for her accident. An accident that everyone at the scene was worried would claim the life of her unborn child.

Lori Bell

She followed behind the ambulance in her own car. She wanted to ride in the ambulance, but she couldn't abandon her car and Sarah Loft had lost full consciousness as she was being loaded into the back of the emergency vehicle. Tasha prayed so hard all the way to the hospital. As she drove, she paid close attention to her surroundings this time with both of her hands tightly gripped to the steering wheel, but she was speeding in order to keep up with the ambulance. All the while, she kept thinking of Jack. And finally, she spoke aloud to him. *Hey, I'm sure you've made it to heaven by now since your soul is as good as gold.* Tasha felt herself wanting to smile. Just the thought of him makes her feel good. *I need a favor. Tell God to keep her and her baby safe. It doesn't matter whose baby it is. It deserves to live.*

***

An hour had gone by since Tasha was directed to a waiting room in the hospital. She thought maybe she had been forgotten about since she is not next of kin to Sarah Loft or anything comparably close to her. Tasha didn't know what to do. She had tried calling Harrison, but he was tied up with a court case and could not be reached. She couldn't keep sitting there, waiting. She needed to know what is happening. As she stood up in the crowded waiting area, a doctor appeared in the doorway. "Tasha Wheelan," he raised his voice over the talking noise and she quickly walked over to him as she caught his eye. He led her out into the hallway

Timing

and she felt nervous awaiting the news he was about to share with her.

"The baby is fine, six weeks early so his lungs are a bit underdeveloped but he is a trooper." The doctor wanted to say *considering the trauma to his mother today*, but he refrained.

"Alright, my goodness, it's a boy and everyone is okay." Tasha didn't know what else to say. She felt beyond relieved, considering she caused the accident.

"Actually that is why I have pulled you aside, there is more…" The doctor's tone was very serious, and his voice seemed shaky as he told Tasha the baby's mother died in the ambulance en route to the hospital. She had lost a lot of blood and had extensive damage to her internal organs, including numerous punctures from a broken spine. But it was her head injury, a fractured skull which he believed took her life. The doctor told her it was an impact injury that shattered the skull, driving fragments of bone into the brain. Tasha could see his lips moving, but she no longer could hear the words coming from his mouth. And suddenly everything went black.

***

She woke up with wet cloths placed on her forehead and behind her neck. She immediately realized she was lying on a gurney in the emergency room. "It's okay honey, you just fainted. You are gonna be just fine." Tasha opened her eyes to an overweight nurse hovering over her. Her make-up was pasty and the color didn't match her skin tone and her breath smelled like peppermint trying to cover up the stale aftermath of cigarette smoke.

The nurse backed away and Tasha was able to breathe through her nose again without feeling queasy. She asked Tasha to remain lying down for a few more minutes before she tried to sit up, or get up. Tasha did as she said and that's when she noticed a woman sitting in a chair against the far wall, staring. Tasha remembered her. She has seen her before. She was the lead emergency medical technician at the scene of the accident. She was with Sarah Loft in the back of the ambulance. When she died.

"Hi...I heard...she... did not make it." As Tasha spoke, her eyes welled up with tears as she thought of that baby without its mother. The doctor had said a boy. She thought of Spence. What a joy it has been for her to have a son. A little boy. Sarah Loft will now never know that kind of joy. Tasha wanted to cry. She wanted to scream as loud and as hard as she possibly could about how *unfair* this is! If she had only one wish right at this moment it would be to reverse her mistake to prevent the accident and the death of Sarah Loft. How incredibly sad. And impossible to deal with. She caused the accident that killed *her*. No one knew it, and it was an unbearably painful truth to accept.

Timing

The woman walked over to Tasha's bedside and her voice was barely more than a whisper. "My name is Kerrigan, I was with her when she passed, she knew she was not going to survive. She drifted in and out of consciousness several times, but she was able to relay a message for me to give you." *A message?* The first thing that came to Tasha's mind is *the baby is Harrison's. Sarah Loft had to have known for certain.* Tasha remained silent, listening, readying herself to hear what she believes she has known all along. "She wants you to have the baby. She was weak and her words were sporadic, but I'm certain of her wishes. She said *please tell her my baby has no one else. Please raise him and love him like your own.*"

Tasha could not process all of this. Not yet. Everything had happened too quickly. Jack is dead. She caused a car accident and now Sarah Loft is dead, but her baby survived after an emergency cesarean section. And, now, this woman, the EMT from the scene of the accident, is telling her the baby boy is hers to keep. *Love him as your own? Was that the true message from her? Is that baby, by blood, her husband's?* "I'm sorry, I don't know what to say right now," Tasha said, trying to sit up on the hospital gurney.

"I understand. You're in shock. It truly is awful what happened." Kerrigan seemed sincere to Tasha, but she also seemed through with her mission to deliver a dying woman's message as if it was just all in a day's work for her and she began to back out of the room. "After you have time to think all of this through, you may want to take a peek at that baby boy in the nursery, but be warned it's love at first sight." The woman, probably in her late twenties and a little on the chubby-side, winked at her as she left the room. She must have thought it was that easy, Tasha thought. *She had absolutely no idea.*

    Tasha's body was shaking. Minus her coat, she was sitting there fully clothed and feeling so chilled as her entire body reacted. She pulled her knees up to her chest, hugged them tightly, and began crying. No one knew she caused that accident. She is responsible for killing a pregnant woman and leaving a baby without a mother. Not just any mother though. Sarah Loft was possibly the mother of Harrison's baby. What choice did she have now? She has to make sure that baby boy is taken care of. Tasha remembered Ari mentioning Sarah Loft has a sister, and an estranged mother who could surface again and claim rights to the baby. Someone will want him. But, that was not Sarah Loft's wish. But, really, what did she owe the woman who was once her husband's mistress? Maybe a few hours ago her answer would have been *not a damn thing*, but now everything had changed. Tasha put her feet on the floor and started walking. She wanted to see that baby boy.

CHAPTER 25

Tasha found the maternity ward. She told them she is the woman who came upon the car accident today, she mentioned the mother dying and the baby surviving. For the most part, she told the truth. The whole truth pained her and so she desperately kept trying to put it out of her head because she knew what she had to do now. She wanted to see the baby, and there was no other way around telling the hospital staff exactly that.

"Look, I don't know what is going to happen," Tasha told the young nurse, "but I need to see him. I need to know he is going to be okay."

Lori Bell

The nurse sympathized with Tasha, coming upon that accident had to be traumatic and every staff member on that hospital floor felt terrible knowing the baby's mother had died. None of them knew about the dying mother's request.

They all just assumed a family member would claim him very soon. The nurse explained to Tasha how the baby is in the neonatal intensive care unit on oxygen to help his lungs to develop, and it is going to take awhile for the baby to learn how to coordinate his breathing and eating, which meant an extended hospital stay.

Tasha followed the nurse's instructions to put on the provided gown, a mask, and gloves. She suited up and walked into the NICU. It was quiet as he was the only baby in there. When Tasha saw a little body inside the transparent incubator, she walked closer and saw him stretch his legs high into the air. So tiny. The nurse said he weighed five pounds, three ounces at birth, and explained how that is pretty good considering he is one month early. Tasha stared at him, without moving any closer. He had the same little scrunched up face that all newborns have. His skin tone looked fair and he had very light blond hairs sticking up about a half an inch all over his little head. Tasha smiled and giggled out loud. Kerrigan, the EMT, was right. *He is something else.*

A nurse walked into the room behind Tasha, a different one than before, and she told her she could put her hands inside the incubator as long as she was wearing gloves.

Timing

She said the baby has a pretty strong grip on a finger already. Tasha hesitated, but then she put her right hand inside the hole. She took his tiny clamped fist into her hand. The baby immediately relaxed, opened his palm and when Tasha put her finger inside of it, he held on for dear life. It was almost as if he knew. Or, maybe it was solely Tasha who felt their connection. Their need to be together. Either way, she could not get that sensation out of her mind, or her heart, when she left the hospital a short time later.

***

She didn't know how she was going to tell him, but she swore to herself that she would tell him the truth. Tasha waited for Spence to go to bed before she made her way upstairs to find Harrison sitting up in their bed, once again reading over a case. That is his ritual almost every night, especially when he is due in court the next day. Court is where he had been all day long and the reason Tasha had not been able to reach him and lean on him in her time of crisis. She made it through homework with Spence after school and dinnertime with both of them, but now she needed to get this out. She was still feeling shaken as she was about to tell Harrison how that baby boy was born today.

"Hi there," Tasha said, carrying a glass of chardonnay into her bedroom. She drank half of it just walking up the stairs to boost her courage or at least take the edge off for the unbelievable story she was about to tell him. Harrison looked up from the laptop resting on his legs. He rarely worked on that laptop at home, in fact Tasha liked to tease him about being old school and having paper copies of everything.

"You okay?" he asked her as she sat down on the end of the bed at his feet.

"Not really," she answered. "I tried to get ahold of you today. Something happened. Something crazy…" Harrison was looking at her. She had his undivided attention now. *Just tell him.* "I went to the cemetery today," Tasha didn't say *to visit her mother's grave* and Harrison instantly wondered if she went there to see Jack. It was too damn frigid outside to stand at a gravesite. "I found out that Jack Williams died of heart disease." It made her feel incredible sadness as she could not fathom how he is gone. Harrison's eyes widened, "First his father and now him? Wow."

"Yes, it was a shock to his family, apparently, and to me. Harrison, I really cared about him. He was there for me when…"

"I know," Harrison interrupted.

Tasha took a deep breath before she continued. "I was upset and driving. I was not paying attention. I was on the frontage road and came to the bend… and I crossed the center line. I was in the direct path of another car and then I came to my senses soon enough to swerve out of the way and back into my lane, and I eventually managed to stop my car on the

Timing

shoulder."

"Oh my God, Tash!" Harrison was alarmed. "What in the hell were you thinking? And you're alright?"

"I am. But, the other driver is not. She panicked, swerved away from me, hit the guard rail and flipped her car. She was not wearing her seatbelt, so she was thrown out of her car." Tasha held both of her hands up to her mouth and began crying. "It was awful, Harrison. I caused that accident on the same road my mother was killed on. I am to blame for it."

"Did anyone call the police?" Harrison was wondering why he was not contacted and he was upset to first be hearing about it now. Little did he know, there was more. Much more.

"I called an ambulance and a police officer did arrive on the scene. I know this is wrong but I was panicked and scared and so I only told them I came upon the accident. No one else was around, so no one knows I caused it."

"Oh Tash…" Harrison put his face in his hands and rubbed his temple bones on the side of his head.

"I know...but once I saw the severity of her injuries, I could not own up to doing that to her and her unborn child. I was just so scared."

"What? The woman is pregnant?"

"She was. The baby was born by emergency c-section today. A boy."

"So all is good with them then, right?"

"The woman died in the ambulance on the way to the hospital." Tasha broke down again. Harrison's face grew pale. He dropped the laptop onto the bed and stood up and came over to her. Sitting beside her, he cradled her in his arms and he could feel her trembling. He felt shocked and he could not imagine how Tasha is going to handle knowing a woman is dead because of her carelessness.

"There's more..." Tasha said, pulling away from Harrison's embrace. "The woman who was driving the other car, the woman who died was... Sarah Loft." At that moment even the lightest touch could have knocked Harrison off of the bed and onto the floor. He was beyond stunned. His shoulders were slumped and his face was back into his hands. Tasha watched him in silence, not knowing what he is thinking. *Did he care about her? Was he worried about what will happen to the baby?* Actually, all he could focus on is how his plan to write off Sarah Loft and her child is no longer feasible. He did not want to know if that baby is his, and now he wondered how in the world he could get out of this mess. He still didn't want to take a paternity test.

"That's terrible," he said, feeling stressed about what will happen now. "I'm assuming she had a will of some sort that states what she would like to see happen to her baby."

Timing

Spoken like a true lawyer, Tasha thought as she answered him bluntly. "She told the EMT in the ambulance that she wanted me to have him."

"What? Oh my God, here we fucking go! Do not fall for this, Tash. That baby is not mine. We are not obligated to raise it. Yes, it's unfortunate she died but my God we should not have to suffer for the rest of our lives!" Harrison's anger surfaced and Tasha was quick to point out the obvious.

"We do not know anything for sure but what I do know is that I am to blame for this. I caused her death. I feel like I need to do this to redeem myself."

"In whose eyes? No one knows!" Harrison was up off of the bed and raising his voice way too loudly for having Spence asleep just down the hallway.

"In my eyes." Tasha felt sick to her stomach. Dear God, what had she done?

"Stop this guilt. Do not change your life, our lives, over this accident because *it was an accident.*"

"But the baby is real, he is here for a reason. I was on that road for a reason. I now see that Jack and my mother were on that road for a reason too. Timing sucks sometimes, but some good can come out of this. We can give that baby, whether he is yours or not, a home."

"Absolutely not!" There was no question about the

words he screamed at his wife before he walked out of their bedroom, slamming the door behind him.

***

She waited for him to calm down. About an hour had passed before she walked down the stairs and found him sitting in the dark on the very bottom step.

She sat down beside him. "I know you're in disbelief about everything I told you. I am, too."

"I don't want that baby, Tash. I never did," he admitted. "It was not just Sarah Loft who I did not want to have in any part of my life, our lives, it's also that baby. I don't want the paternity test. I am going to tell you something and you may see me as the worst person in the world when I do, but it's the truth. It will make you see how strongly I feel about not wanting that baby." Tasha was listening intently and would never have admitted it aloud to her husband, but his words were scaring her. "I called her shortly after we found out she was pregnant. She came to my office and I made her an offer she didn't refuse." Harrison was not looking at Tasha while he spoke to her, he kept looking down at the floor, at his bare feet planted there. They were sitting close enough for her to hear his heavy breathing. He was nervous about telling her this. "I was going to pay her one million dollars to say this baby is not mine. I did not want

Timing

a paternity test, I still don't and I most certainly do not want that baby."

It was Tasha's turn to be shocked and angry. "Well it's no wonder now why you were so fucking adamant about the baby *not* being yours! How could you, Harrison? And how can you now? Don't you see what is happening here? We were about to be at a crossroads in our relationship with that baby on the way. I had doubts our marriage would survive if that baby turned out to be yours. You didn't want to face it, and I dreaded the day it would be born. Well, that day is here, and nothing is happening the way either of us imagined or, in your case, secretly planned for it to be. You were going to pay her off in order to save our marriage? Now I'm asking you to help me get custody of the baby. Use money and your resources as an attorney to make it happen. It's the right thing to do, and it could very well be exactly what you and I need."

"What we need is for this nightmare to be over!" Harrison said, turning to look at his wife and placing his hands firmly on her shoulders. "Let it go. Let this crazy idea go."

"I can't," were the only words she replied as she pulled out of his grip, stood up, and walked back up the stairs.

CHAPTER 26

Tasha spent the entire next week at the hospital. The staff had gotten used to her showing up and staying with the baby all day long. She held him for the first time on the second day she visited and then she asked to help with feeding him. By the week's end, Tasha was allowed to give him his first bath. He was getting stronger sooner than anyone expected and Tasha was told he may not have to stay in the hospital for the originally projected month.

Timing

No one yet had come to visit him. If Sarah Loft's family was aware of her death, no one wanted to claim her baby. As Tasha increasingly attached herself to the baby, she got caught up in the notion that she would be the one to bring him home. Otherwise, he had no place to go. And one of the nurses in the NICU inquired about it when she and Tasha were alone.

"So what is this little guy's story? This sweet yet-to-be named baby boy, who any one of us here would take home in a heartbeat, does not have a home to go to. We are assuming it's you, because we have heard the rumors. His mother was dying at the scene of the car accident you witnessed and she wanted you to have him. Doesn't the baby have a father or any family who wants him? And will you honor a stranger's dying wish?" Tasha had gotten to know all of the nurses and she liked them, this one in particular, so she did not mind her straightforwardness. But, Tasha herself didn't have any definite answers to any of those questions right now. She wants to bring that baby boy home, she wants to be the one to name him and raise him, but there are roadblocks in the way of that actually happening. Her husband is the main barrier.

Harrison had again become distant and cold again toward her. She told him where she was each day and what she did all day long, and he had no response. She told him that many babies born with underdeveloped lungs grow to be healthy and function normally. Some, however, have long-term effects such as developing asthma or breathing difficulties or can be more prone to pneumonia. This baby, however, is showing no signs of having any difficulties. He is still being kept in an incubator and would be for at least a couple more weeks. She explained how the incubator is basically the making of an artificial uterus for the baby to live in until he is developed enough to survive on his own. Harrison didn't even appear to be listening when Tasha told him how the baby has a tube giving him oxygen and it does the job of his lungs for him until they have developed, and every few hours the nurses do an exercise where they tap his chest and it helps his lungs learn how to function. Tasha was completely caught up in everything about that baby. She considered every tiny step of his progress an answered prayer.

It was late on a Friday night and Spence was at a school dance. At almost eleven years old, he swore he would not be asking a girl to dance. He only wanted to go to *be cool and hang out with his buddies.* Tasha smiled to herself as she was thinking about her son. And then she thought about the baby boy. She wanted to go see him again over the weekend, and she knew it was a long shot, *hell it was inconceivable at this point*, but she wanted Harrison to go along with her.

They were sitting in their living room when she brought up the notion to him. He pretended to be intently watching a football game between the St. Louis Rams and the

Timing

Green Bay Packers when Tasha stood up in front of their flat screen television on the wall which resembled that of a small-screen movie theater. She had his attention away from the game now and he looked up at her with sincerity again. "So is this the part where you demand I have that paternity test done? And if I finally agree, will you give up on this quest to make him yours?"

"I don't care if you ever have the test. That is not what this is about anymore," Tasha stated. "This is about that baby needing love, and needing us. Just come with me, see him, and you will feel what I do."

"No. And don't ever ask me to again." Tasha stood in front of him for a few more seconds before she gave up. She was again looking at the man who could be hurtful and heartless. She thought those days were behind them, but she was wrong.

***

Tasha was on a mission when she visited the hospital the following day. She found her favorite nurse and inquired about what happens to babies left there in the hospital without parents or other relatives to claim them. Tasha learned exactly what she feared were true. The babies are placed into the custody of the state and are taken into the foster care system. There is a period of time that has to pass for claims by either the parent or family members. After that time has passed, the child is available for adoption through the foster care system.

    Tasha wanted to take him home. She, after all, was Sarah Loft's choice in the end to take care of him and be his mother. That, unfortunately, was not in writing but there was a witness, Kerrigan, the EMT. Tasha wanted to track her down and get her statement but in order to do that, she needed an attorney. And that is when she called Thomas-Wheelan Law Firm and asked for John Thomas. John knew Sarah Loft was Harrison's mistress and how she had gotten pregnant. John hesitated to help Tasha behind Harrison's back, but he did agree to make a few phone calls. An hour and a half later, he had some answers for Tasha.

    "Today is your lucky day, kid," he said to her when she picked up her cell phone after the first ring. She walked out into the hospital hallway because the baby was sleeping in his incubator. She had just fed him, and could still smell his sweet scent on her gown she was wearing over top of her clothes. "There is no need for you to get the EMT's statement, because I tracked down Ms. Loft's attorney and found out she had her ducks in a row. She has a will, and *Harrison* is listed to have sole custody if she were to pass. She apparently just recently planned her living will in fear of dying during childbirth because her pregnancy did have its complications." Tasha could not believe how easy this had become. "So, all

Timing

you have to do is get your husband to sign the papers, which have been faxed to me already, and you can take that baby home." Tasha was smiling and tears were rolling down her cheeks. She thanked John profusely and he was laughing on the other end of the phone as he said, "Congratulations, mama."

***

As Tasha was about to leave the hospital, feeling empowered and determined to convince Harrison to sign the papers waiting on his desk in his office, she made her way out into the hallway and was slipping off her gown when she heard a voice behind her.

"Mrs. Wheelan?"

Tasha turned to find a young woman, probably close to Ari's age, standing there. "Yes, hi," she said.

"I am Kate Loft, Sarah's sister." Tasha froze. She went to high school with Ari. She is the baby's aunt, and suddenly Tasha was afraid her chance of taking him home with her is now over.

"Oh Kate, honey, I'm very sorry for your loss." Tasha meant those words more than that young woman would ever know. She still felt terrible pangs of guilt when she thought about what happened, when she allowed herself to relive that accident. The accident she caused. The life she is responsible for taking.

"Thank you," Kate said, looking sad and a little bit lost. "I know you've been here with my nephew. I came here once to see him." Tasha had no idea, but she remained silent as Kate continued speaking. "I know Sarah wanted you to have him." Here is the moment Tasha was dreading. A family member will claim the baby and take him away. Tasha didn't know if she was strong enough to watch this happen. "I just want you to know that I speak for myself and my mother when I say thank you from the very bottom of our hearts for what you're doing. He needs a good home, and I have heard here in this hospital how you want to give that to him."

Tasha was not sure if she heard her right. Sarah Loft's family didn't want him? She is, again, free to have him? This just seemed too easy. Except for Harrison putting up his fight, this seemed like it is meant to happen. "So your mother does not want to be in his life?" Tasha held her breath after she spoke those words. "No. She and my sister were estranged and…is there somewhere we can go to talk?" Kate asked Tasha and she immediately suggested coffee in the cafeteria.

After they settled at a table in the busy cafeteria, Kate spoke first. "My mother was embarrassed and ashamed of Sarah. She was, as you know, very promiscuous. My mother does not want the baby, and I don't have the time or the money to keep him. I am in college and I want a life for

Timing

myself. I would like to know how he's doing now and then, if that is not too much to ask..." It had not felt official or even like a reality for Tasha until this very moment. She is going to be that baby boy's mother. She had the say-so in everything now. She felt grateful and blessed. It all felt meant to be. Harrison would come around, she just knew it.

"Of course," Tasha said, "I should be the one thanking you, and your mother. I want your sister's baby. I already love him as my own." She spoke those words and she truly meant them.

The two of them talked at length about the baby, and eventually about Sarah Loft. It was no secret that Tasha was not fond of her. She was her husband's mistress, and that was enough said. But, Kate had more to say.

"I know your husband could be the baby's father. I actually talked to my sister about the possible men who could be..."

"How many were there?" Tasha just flat out asked Sarah Loft's sister that burning question. "I mean, was she sure about one over another being the father?"

"She told me only your husband or one other man could be the father. She knew who she was with and when that particular month her baby was conceived. I think she wanted the baby's father to be your husband because he was not her one night stand. She was with the other guy only one time." Tasha was listening carefully and actually found herself hoping Harrison is the father. Crazy how life works. Everything had since done a one hundred and eighty degree turn in her mind and now in her heart. "She described the other man as someone she hooked up with after they met and drank together in a bar downtown, the one on Main, I think," Kate said, and Tasha nodded her head, but she was incapable of imagining picking up a man, a stranger at a bar and allowing him to touch her and share that kind of intimacy. "She didn't even know his name, but that wasn't a shocker," Kate continued, "All she said is he was a gentleman compared to most of the men she's been with…and this is strange but she said he lived at the cemetery, like behind it or something. Wild, isn't it?" Kate's words trailed off and Tasha did not hear anything else from there on. *Behind the cemetery. There is only one house on the hill. A gentleman. The bar on Main. For the love of God…Jack could be the baby's father.*

CHAPTER 27

It was timing at its best. It was the *impeccable* timing Jack had told her about. She heard his words ringing in her ears as she drove home. *The timing in which God sets everything in motion on this earth is impeccable. He brought us together for a reason. Don't lose sight of that.*

Suddenly it all made sense. The day they met. The closeness they immediately shared. The baby on the way. The pain of discovering Jack had died. The absolute understanding of what Jack went through when he crossed the center line in his truck and killed her mother because she had done the very same thing on that exact road.

She ached knowing she will never see him again. But, maybe, just maybe, this baby is the part of Jack she will be able to have and to hold for the rest of her life. It was meant to be. She is meant to have Jack's baby now that he is gone. Tasha felt certain that baby boy she already loves has Jack's blood running through his veins. That would explain her instantaneous bond with him.

First, she broke the news to Harrison that the papers are legit and ready to be signed, because Sarah Loft was actually on top of things. And then he came unglued. "You have got to be kidding me! Now you're in cahoots with John?" He was standing in the middle of their kitchen and she was seated at the table.

"No, I am not. I simply asked him for his help because you've been a son of a bitch about all of this. Harrison, you know I have to act now before the state takes him. At least I know I have rights to him, or you do. Please don't fight me on this anymore. Let's get in the car and go get those papers in your office and sign them and we will file them and bring him home soon."

"Do you even hear yourself?" Harrison was glaring at her.

"Yes, but you don't seem to hear me anymore."

"That's because you're so consumed with guilt that you can't think straight. This is real life, and that baby will fuck up ours if you go through with this. Tash, we don't even know who fathered him. If I didn't, it could be some druggie and we could deal with those kinds of genes for the rest of our lives." Tasha immediately thought of Jack. *Yes, this baby could have his daddy's genes.*

Timing

"Harrison, I've thought about all of that and I don't care about the odds of having troubles down the road. Sign the papers or I am going to ask you to draw up our divorce papers." She surprised herself with that comment. She had spoken in anger, in desperation. She didn't mean it. She didn't want to divorce him, that used to be the last thing she ever wanted. She felt like the two of them had finally fought their way back to each other the last several months, but right now she didn't care about saving what they gave their all to get back. Their marriage was no longer her top priority. The baby is.

"You're not serious?" Harrison felt scared, but his anger overpowered his fear of losing her this time. "You're choosing a baby over me, over us? I *will* divorce you before I ever agree to this absurdity of yours. Keep the kid. I will sign him over to you, and then I will sign off on our marriage. I'm done." He walked away feeling shaken and uncertain. She was left sitting in their home, in their kitchen, feeling exactly the same. She had lost her husband over a baby. That baby ended up destroying their marriage after all.

CHAPTER 28

Tasha spent the following two weeks getting ready. She turned a vacant room in their house, which used to be a playroom for Spence when they first moved in, into a nursery. She bought everything from bottles, formula and diapers to furniture – a crib, a dresser and rocker – and all of the necessary baby gear including a bouncy seat, car seat and stroller. She also had fun buying little soft sleepers, mostly in all shades of blue, for the baby to wear for the remaining winter months in Baltimore. The weather had been more frigid than previous ones, so Tasha was ready to keep *her* little one warm. She still couldn't believe it. She was giddy at the thought of it, but also at the same time she was very worried about her marriage. Harrison had not brought up the prospect of divorce to her again, and she had not either. They were still living in the same house with their son, but once again they were disconnected.

Timing

Harrison saw what his wife was doing to ready for a baby to move into their house and take over their lives. Tasha had explained to her children that a baby in the hospital needed a home and she was going to adopt him. Ari, on the phone from college, thought her mother's decision was *bananas,* but in the next breath she expressed her excitement about meeting *the little guy* the next time she is on break and able to come home. Spence was more confused about his mother's desire to bring a child who is not *hers* into their home. Tasha did her best to explain to him it is something she feels compelled to do, and then her son surprised her with his words. *"What about me? I'm your son. Will you still have time for me?"* Tasha did her best to reassure him, but she didn't feel like she got through to him. Just like with Harrison.

Tasha was in the garage trying to figure out how to properly install the car seat base into the backseat of her car. She read the instructions but was still struggling with securing it when Harrison came home. He had seen the empty box and its contents on the floor of his side of the garage so he refrained from pulling his car inside. After he parked his car outside on the driveway, he walked into the garage and closed the door to keep the cold air out as he watched his wife. He remembered being the one who always installed things like that when their kids were babies. He also had put together all of the gear, including the crib. He had not reached out to help Tasha at all in the last couple of weeks and he wanted to keep it that way. He just wanted to leave, but it just wasn't that easy for him because he still wanted her and their family to stay together. He hoped with every fiber of his being that Tasha would not go through with the adoption. Knowing that tomorrow is the day she is supposed to bring the baby home and into their lives, he wanted to try one more time to convince her not to do it.

"Are you having trouble with that?" he asked her as he walked over to the counter by the sink and set his briefcase on it. Tasha was a bit caught off guard by the kindness in his eyes at the moment. He has been avoiding her and appearing angry at her for weeks. "Um, yeah, will you help me do this the correct way?" Harrison took off his overcoat, set it on the driver's seat, and then rolled up the long sleeves on his white dress shirt to his elbows. He loosened his powder blue tie and then bent down to take a look into the car.

"You're doing it right, it just needs to be pulled tighter to keep the base secure and in place for when you attach the car seat to it. Gotta keep that little guy safe." After he secured the base, he was backing out of the car when Tasha stepped close to him, putting her fingers through the belt loops in his dress pants and she said, "Thank you."

"I don't want you to do this, Tash." Harrison admitted.

"And I don't want you to distance yourself from me again like you've been doing for weeks. We can't go back to being miserable in our marriage."

Timing

"We are not going to have a marriage if you bring that baby home tomorrow."

***

The papers had already been filed for Tasha to adopt him, but Harrison wanted no part of it. He had signed over the rights Sarah Loft granted him in her will, and he signed them over to his wife. She looked into her rearview mirror as she drove away from the hospital. For safety, infant car seats had to be turned around, facing the back of the car so Tasha had strapped a small kiddie mirror with frogs on it to the top of the backseat so she could see him as she drove them home. The baby boy in tow has a name now. Lance Harrison Wheelan. Tasha had chosen Lance, without question, because without Jackson Lance Williams III that baby boy would not be in her life right now. Did she believe Jack is his biological father? She didn't know for certain. She had quickly warmed to the possibility, but wanted to keep Lance no matter what. She wanted to believe that God's plan was for Jack to waltz in her life, and change it for the better. And then, when he had to leave this earth so suddenly, his baby would be left behind for Tasha to love for the rest of her life. It felt meant to be. And her reason behind choosing the baby's middle name just felt right also as she was not giving up hope for Harrison to be in Lance's life.

Lori Bell

The baby was sleeping as Tasha lifted the car seat out of the car and carried it into the house and all the way upstairs to the nursery. He remained sleeping while Tasha unbuckled him and carefully scooped him out. *Oh my, it's been a long time since I've felt like this,* Tasha thought to herself as she stood in front of his crib, holding him close and listening to him breathe. *Thank God for those healthy lungs.* Lance checked out perfectly with the pediatrician before he was discharged from the hospital, and Tasha felt so much joy as she welcomed him home today. All by herself.

***

Tasha had the receiving end of the baby monitor sitting on the kitchen counter while she helped Spence with his math homework at the kitchen table. She always helped him with math. Harrison was not home yet and he had not called either. Spence had fun playing with the baby after school, but he admitted how he *wished the baby didn't have to stay with them forever.* Tasha reminded him how, without them, Lance does not have a home. He has no mother or father to care for him. Tasha did not go into too much detail with her son, but she could not bear the thought of the state taking the baby and placing him into foster care. He could easily be passed around too many times or, God forbid, be mistreated. Tasha did not want that kind of life for this baby. She could give him a good life. And she will.

Timing

It was eleven o'clock when Tasha was downstairs in the kitchen again. This time she was rinsing out a bottle in the sink and as she went to set it upside down in the dishwasher, she heard Harrison come inside the door. She kept her back to him, feeling angry. He had not called and she does not know where he's been. This was not going to fly with her anymore. If he was dropping his pants to be with other women again, he could get out.

"Hi," Harrison said as he noticed what she was doing.

"My phone must be broken, I never got your call to say you would be this late." Tasha was tired and not in any mood to have this conversation but she knew she had to. Their marriage had taken a nose dive again in recent weeks and she didn't know if it is salvageable this time, but she did feel stronger than she has ever felt in her life. Strong enough to be a single mother to Ari, Spence, and this new baby. If she had to.

"I worked late," was all Harrison replied as he set his briefcase down on the table and took off his coat, hanging it on the chair. He would put everything in its place later. Right now he wanted to confront his wife about going against his wishes today. "So you did it, huh? You brought that baby into our house today."

"His name is Lance Harrison Wheelan, and he's ours now." Tasha was choosing her words carefully. Legally,

Lance is hers but she wanted Harrison to know he can be theirs. His middle name, in a way, proved he already is.

"No, you mean he's yours." Harrison walked over to her, she was standing with her back against the counter and he stood directly in front of her, toe to toe.

"Biologically, he could be yours." Tasha thought of Jack, but pushed that thought aside as she readied herself to fight for what she believes in.

"I told you, I don't want him either way and you didn't hear me. You didn't want to listen to me when I begged you to leave this alone. I wanted you and *our* family, *our* kids, not the infant of some floozy." Tasha could smell scotch on Harrison's breath.

"Is that what you picked up tonight, another floozy?" Tasha almost spat the words at him. *Damn him.*

"No, I told you I was working late." Harrison defended himself.

"You've been drinking…"

"I had a drink with John before he left the office, and then I poured myself another one. I was alone, Tash. I swear." She believed him.

"Give this a chance, Harry. Walk with me through this. You will see how giving this baby a home is the right

Timing

thing to do. He has no one else. I am responsible for his mother's accident." Tasha cringed at the thought. That truth will always deeply pain her. "He could be yours."

"I was drinking at the office tonight, because I had to draw up our divorce papers," he ignored her plea. "I don't want to lose you, but I can't go along with this crazy idea of yours. I want out." Harrison walked over to his briefcase lying flat on the kitchen table and he opened the front tabs on it and lifted the lid. And when he pulled out the stack of papers, paper clipped together, he handed them to Tasha with tears in his eyes. She refused to take them. She kept both of her hands at her side. He moved past her and set the papers down on the countertop behind her and all she heard him say before he walked away was, "Just sign them."

CHAPTER 29

The divorce papers were inside of a top drawer in the kitchen cabinet. It is a place where they kept loose-leaf paper, pens and pencils, scissors and tape. Tasha had put the document in that drawer and closed it. Two weeks had gone by and she had not opened the drawer again, and the papers remained unsigned.

The baby had consumed her. At forty-five years old, Tasha now knew why women twenty years younger were meant to raise *babies*. Her days revolved around feedings, naps, and keeping Lance content. Forget the gym. Forget all errands. Lance was not a difficult baby to take care of, but he did require more than Tasha was beginning to think she could handle by herself.

Timing

For three consecutive nights, Lance had not been sleeping. He was waking up every fifteen or twenty minutes, crying. He was not hungry, his diaper was dry, he did not appear to be in pain, and Tasha tried everything to sooth him. Most times holding him or rocking him helped. *This is just a phase*, she told herself repeatedly and did so again at two-thirty in the morning. Her body ached from being so tired and Tasha made her way through the dark house and into her bed. When she pulled the sheet and duvet over her body, she realized what she had just done. For several weeks now, even before Lance moved in, Tasha had been sleeping in Ari's bed. She had the baby monitor set up in her daughter's vacant room and it had become *her* room. Tonight, however, Tasha was not thinking clearly as she made her way to her bedroom, practically fell into bed, and realized she was in her bed with Harrison.

Her eyes immediately popped open. She was going to slip back out quickly and quietly before she woke him, but it was too late. Harrison had not been affected by the fussy baby at night, because he was always able to roll over and go back to sleep. It is his wife who he could see this baby is taking a toll on. She no longer made time to work out at the gym, she no longer applied any make up to accent her eyes and her lips every day. She managed to pick up the house, cook dinner, and transport Spence to and from school and sports. Harrison believes his wife is a good mother, he has always believed that. But, seeing her put herself through the mill for a baby which is not even hers annoyed him to no end. It was obvious to him how much she loved the baby and Harrison could see Spence's growing attachment to him as well. He is the only one in that house who felt like a stranger. His family was settling into a new life without him, and so he knew it was time for him to make a decision. Join them. Or leave.

Harrison rolled onto his side and looked at his wife lying beside him. She was flat on her back and she had closed her eyes again and immediately began drifting off to sleep. She knew what she had done, she registered the mistake in her mind and she did intend to get up and out of that bed and move to the other room, but her body gave in to extreme exhaustion and she fell asleep. It was the comfort of being in her own bed again, and maybe it even soothed her to be that close to her husband. Whatever the scenario, Tasha crashed and slept for three consecutive hours.

She never heard the baby crying twenty-two minutes after she fell asleep in bed with Harrison. There was no monitor to alert her, so she remained sound asleep. Harrison was not going to go to him. He hoped the baby would cry it out and fall back to sleep quickly. *Dammit,* he thought to himself, as he considered nudging his wife to wake her so she could take care of the baby again. It was her place to tend to that baby, he thought, because she wanted him. Then he got out of bed, barefoot in his black silk pajama pants, and he left the room.

Timing

***

Tasha began stirring in her sleep. She rolled from her stomach to her back, and began stretching her legs and arms and relishing the feeling of having gotten some good sleep. That is when her eyes popped open. *Good sleep? Not with a baby in the house!* Tasha sat straight up in bed, and again realized being in the wrong bed. Harrison was not in their bed, but she did hear the shower water running in their master bathroom. She jumped up out of bed, practically sprinted down the hallway and into the baby's room. She slowed herself down as she entered the nursery so she would not wake the baby. It surprised her to think he had slept for a few hours straight, and she instantly felt worried.

When she peeked into his crib, she saw the soft little blue Winnie the Pooh blanket that had quickly become a favorite of his for naptime and nighttime, but she did not see the baby. The crib was empty and he was gone.

Tasha did not panic. In fact, she could not move. She just stood there, trying to process this. She instantly thought of Spence and how he had asked her the night before if he could take Lance into his bed to sleep with him. Tasha explained to him how that is not safe for a newborn baby and Lance's crying would wake him too many times all night long. Tasha left the nursery and carefully opened the door to Spence's room. It was early, he still had another two hours to sleep before he had to get ready for school, so Tasha was going to just swoop up the baby and leave the room. She looked once, she looked closer and all she could see was Spence sprawled out and sound asleep. She felt her heartbeat quicken as she pulled back the blankets and then the sheet. She was relieved to see the baby had not been underneath all of those covers, but she found herself rushing out of the room and back into her room. He may not care about the baby, but she had to tell Harrison what is happening. She flung open the bathroom door as shower steam met her in the air. She saw him standing in front of the sink with a thick white towel wrapped low around his waist and shaving cream smeared all over his cheeks and his chin. Only his lips were visible on the bottom half of his face as he turned to look at her. She felt so panicked as she started to speak. "I need your help, the baby–" Just then Tasha looked down at the floor in front of the shower door. Lance was inside of his bouncy seat, kicking wildly as the seat moved with him and he began cooing at her.

"He likes it in here," Harrison said, smiling as shaving cream dripped off of his chin and onto the tile floor at his feet.

"You took him out of his crib?" Tasha asked, not knowing what to think or how to feel at this moment.

"Yes, I did, about three hours ago. You came to our bed, by mistake I think, and you didn't hear the little man screaming for you."

Timing

"You should have woken me."

"I didn't have the heart."

"Thank you… um has he been fed?" Tasha looked at the baby, and then back at her husband. This just felt so right for her. For them.

"Yes. I'm glad you had a bottle ready to mix on the counter because otherwise I never would have figured it out. Guess I have a lot to relearn." Harrison bent over the sink to rinse the remaining shaving cream off of his face.

"What are you saying, Harrison? Do you want to be a part of his life?" Tasha almost held her breath as she remained standing right where she had walked into the bathroom a few minutes earlier.

"I found an apartment this past week. I made the down-payment. I was not going to be a part of this anymore, this idea you have of a family," Harrison's words were intense and Tasha feared the thought of him going that far to prepare to leave her and their family. "I wanted to walk away, but I could not grasp the thought of actually leaving Spence… or being anywhere without you."

Tasha felt her eyes tear up and she remained silent. She had said enough to him the past several weeks to try to bring him on board, to try to make him see they could all be happy together. It was his turn to speak and to share how he feels, and she had hoped with all of her being that his feelings have changed. "When I walked into this little guy's room last night, I felt needed. He stopped crying when I picked him up. It has been so long, I didn't trust myself to pick him up the correct way, but he trusted me. He looked at me with those big, round eyes and I knew I could not walk away."

"Oh my God, Harry..." Tasha finally spoke and she hurried over to him and fell into his arms and she whispered, *Thank you*, as he held her. And when he pulled back from their embrace, he had one more thing to tell her.

"I don't know how I am going to get you to understand this, but I will try." Tasha nodded her head. "I do not want to know if he's mine and the only way I can explain that to you is to tell you how I will always feel terrible regret for cheating on you. I do not need a reminder of that each time I look at this baby. I do not want a child with another woman. I want to share Lance Harrison with you and I want to think of him as ours, not mine from an affair. It's the only way I can forgive myself and move on."

"I understand," Tasha said, looking at her husband and knowing it is time he knew what she knows about the baby. As Lance remained content in his bouncer, Tasha explained to Harrison how she found out that Jack Williams was the only other man who could have fathered the baby. A part of Harrison instantaneously wanted to call it all off. He wanted to get angry and run, but then his wife's words stopped him.

Timing

Tasha explained how she is not holding onto this baby as a memento of a man who got away. She admitted to initially feeling like that, but not anymore. She now sees this baby as a blessing, a part of a plan steadily in place all along. She was meant to meet Jack, and Jack was supposed to ultimately guide her back to her husband. It is because of Jack that Tasha was able to finally see how she desperately needed to make changes in her life. She only needed a push. That push and those changes led her to fight for her marriage. She had finally recognized the courage buried inside of her for far too long and she found her own strength again.

"So many things have gone wrong, so many sad things have happened. Lives have ended. My mother is gone. Jack is gone. Sarah Loft is gone. All of them should have been given more time. I want more time. I want to make this right while I can. This baby is a chance for me to begin again and if you still want to be by my side for the next chapter, then I say let's do this. Together."

CHAPTER 30

Six months later, a For Sale sign was up in the yard and on top of it was the word SOLD.

Tasha backed out of her driveway, one last time. The car was packed with everything she, Spence, and the baby would need for the three-hour drive. Spence was watching his mom's face as her black BMW rolled backwards off the curb. She seemed both happy and sad. It was, nonetheless, a bittersweet moment. "We're leaving behind lots of memories here, buddy," Tasha said to her son sitting beside her in the front passenger seat.

Timing

"Yeah, I know mom, but it's going to feel good to go back home." Tasha agreed with her son. Moving back to Greenville, New York seemed like a dream. When their family moved to Baltimore, Maryland nearly four years ago, their lives were falling apart. Ari and Spence were heartbroken to leave their friends, which was entirely why Ari wanted to return to New York for college to be with some of her friends again. Spence made new friends quickly, but never forgot his old buddies. He was eager to return to growing up with those familiar faces. Harrison made millions of dollars when he joined a partnership with John Thomas' law firm, but he eventually learned how all of that money in his world was not worth sacrificing his family's happiness. It was in part a selfish move then, he knew that now. Tasha had already hired a nanny in Greenville, New York to help her take care of Lance because she had put the plans in motion to resurrect her home design business. She ran that company when her first two children were small and she would do it again while raising Lance. That business had part of her heart. With it, she wanted to channel her creativity and find her self-worth again.

As Tasha drove her boys out of the City of Baltimore, she began to tuck away all of the memories, one by one. Some of those memories harbored pain and loss and the overall fear of being alone. Others, had found a way into her heart and they would not only be memories for her, but treasures. As she drove on the frontage road and around the bend, she thought of her mother… she thought of Sarah Loft… and finally, when she passed the cemetery entrance, she thought of Jack Williams. He was an angel now and she knew, without a doubt, she could count on his guardianship for the rest of her life.

Tasha looked into her rearview mirror and smiled at the sight of her sleeping baby in his car seat. And then she looked ahead at the full-sized moving truck driving in front of her with a silver BMW in tow. She had most definitely come full circle with him. She beamed at the thought of embarking on a new adventure because, without a doubt, she was certain she would follow that man anywhere.

ABOUT THE AUTHOR

Many times when I am at particular places, I people watch. Sometimes I don't even realize I'm doing it, but I'm one of those people who simply enjoys looking at what other people are wearing, how they are acting, or even observing how well they (do or do not) take care of their bodies, their hair, etc. Last spring, my husband and I attended a graduation ceremony which took place in a high school gymnasium. We did not have either one of our children along with us, so I was able to completely engross myself in people watching. And what I witnessed inspired me to write TIMING.

There was a woman, in her fifties I guessed, who entered the gymnasium walking a few steps behind a man, who I assumed was her husband. What struck me first was the way that this particular woman was following him. She appeared submissive and that immediately made me feel uneasy. First, if a man is any kind of a gentleman, he allows a woman to walk in front of him. While he continued walking, I watched the woman behind him turn to the bleachers and eye the empty second row from the bottom and she stopped her husband from walking by using her voice. She suggested they sit down in that open row, because the gymnasium was already crowded. As she climbed up the bleachers and sat down, the man she was with obviously spotted someone he knew about twenty or thirty feet in front of him, so he left her sit and proceeded to walk over to talk to his friend (or acquaintance) already seated on the bleachers. I looked at the woman, sitting there alone, and she appeared crushed. She looked over at the man she was with and back down at her lap. She did this about ten times within a few minutes. In the midst of looking and probably wondering if he was going to ask her to move from where she was seated or rejoin her, I saw tears welling up in her eyes. It was at that moment that I thought to myself, how sad, how rude. The man eventually returned to her and he told her in very matter-of-fact terms that they were not sitting where she had already sat down and placed her handbag beside her. Even after she explained how the air flow was better near the door in the already steamy-feeling gymnasium, he wanted to move, and she obliged. It appeared to me like she was following orders and wouldn't dare disobey him. Especially in public.

When that couple walked away, I never saw them again. I did not know who they were, and still to this day I have no idea. I do know from those few minutes of observation, I was inspired. I was inspired to write the character, Tasha Wheelan. I saw a woman dressed to the nines with her make-up applied flawlessly and not a root was showing on her head of highlighted white-blonde hair. On the outside, she appeared extremely put together. Maybe that was her façade, to look the part in an attempt to hide the pain or unhappiness. Maybe she was okay with the way that man (probably her husband) was treating her, or just accustomed to it. And so the character of Tasha was born.

As the story of TIMING begins, we see a woman in a very black and white situation. As the story unfolds, we see the gray. We see a woman who truly is torn about staying in her marriage and fighting harder than she ever has before, or finally walking away. We see a woman who needs to find her strength, and I believe Tasha did. Page after page.

Some relationships are effortless, some are complicated. No connection is exactly the same, but what we should all be striving for in any relationship is mutual respect, mutual love, and happiness. As an author, I want to write happy endings in all of my books. I think every reader wants to see a happy ending. As for real life, the choice is ours to be happy. Work at it, strive for it, seize it. And that is my wish for all of you...be good to yourself, surround yourself with people who are good to you, and find *your* happiness.

Thank you for reading!

love,

Lori Bell

Made in the USA
San Bernardino, CA
20 October 2014